'We were never fr...

'I am glad you agree,' A... not friends; we were lovers. Like me, you cannot forget what we shared.'

'We didn't share anything,' Abby broke in desperately. 'I wish you'd just leave me alone.'

'Do you? Is that what your brother wishes also?'

'Leave Edward out of this.'

'Unfortunately, I cannot.' Alejandro gave a regretful sigh. 'Is that not why he has sent for you? Because he hopes you may succeed where he has failed?'

Abby stiffened. 'Failed?' she echoed. 'Failed at what?'

'Ah…' Alejandro sounded as if her confusion had pleased him. 'You do not know.'

'Know what?'

'That is for me to know and you to find out. So…you will have dinner with me tomorrow evening. We will continue this discussion then, *no*?'

'No!'

'Oh, I think you will, *cara*.'

New York Times bestselling author **Anne Mather** has written since she was seven, but it was only when her first child was born that she fulfilled her dream of becoming a writer. Her first book, CAROLINE, appeared in 1966. It met with immediate success, and since then Anne has written more than 140 novels, reaching a readership which spans the world.

Born and raised in the north of England, Anne still makes her home there with her husband, two children and, now, grandchildren. Asked if she finds writing a lonely occupation, she replies that her characters always keep her company. In fact, she is so busy sorting out their lives that she often doesn't have time for her own! An avid reader herself, she devours everything from sagas and romances to mainstream fiction and suspense. Anne has also written a number of mainstream novels, with DANGEROUS TEMPTATION, her most recent title, published by MIRA® Books.

Recent titles by the same author:

HOT PURSUIT
HIS VIRGIN MISTRESS
THE SPANIARD'S SEDUCTION

ALEJANDRO'S REVENGE

BY
ANNE MATHER

*First published in Great Britain 2003
Harlequin Mills & Boon Limited,
Eton House, 18-24 Paradise Road, Richmond, Surrey TW9 1SR*

© Anne Mather 2003

ISBN 0 263 83222 8

*Set in Times Roman 10 on 11 pt.
01-0403-57695*

*Printed and bound in Spain
by Litografía Rosés, S.A., Barcelona*

CHAPTER ONE

THE car radio was droning on and on about the temperature in Miami, the highs and lows, the relative humidity. But actually Abby was finding it anything but relative. And heat, or the lack of it, was a subjective thing anyway.

When she'd stepped out of the shadows of the airport buildings half an hour ago she'd been dazzled by the sunlight. Perspiration had soon been trickling down her spine and between her breasts. Now, in the air-conditioned luxury of the limousine, she was practically freezing, and all she really wanted to do was reach her destination and lie down until the throbbing in her head subsided.

But that wasn't going to happen. Not any time soon anyway. The arrival of the limousine, which surely couldn't be Edward's property, seemed to prove that. Instead of Lauren being there to meet her she'd been faced with a blank-faced chauffeur who, apart from the necessary introductions, seemed unable—or unwilling—to indulge in polite conversation.

At first she hadn't been concerned. The roads leading away from the airport had been jammed with traffic, and when her swarthy driver had turned off the main thoroughfare to thread his way through a maze of streets only a native of Miami would recognise she'd assumed he was taking a short cut to the hospital.

Which just went to show that you shouldn't take anything for granted, she thought uneasily. Although they'd rejoined the freeway, she was fairly sure they were heading away from the city and South Dade Memorial Hospital where her brother was lying, injured, waiting for her to rush to his bedside. What little she recalled of her first and only other visit to the area was convincing her that they were heading into Coral Gables.

And the only people she knew who lived in Coral Gables were Lauren's parents.

And Alejandro Varga, her treacherous memory reminded her unkindly, but she ignored it.

Still, if they were going to the Esquivals' home then she would just have to put up with it. And at least they'd be able to tell her how serious Edward's injuries were. Perhaps Lauren was staying with them while her husband was in hospital. She hadn't thought to ask any questions when Edward had called her.

Concentrating her attention on her surroundings, she looked through tinted windows at a scene straight out of a travel ad. The broad tree-lined avenue they were driving along ran parallel with the glistening waters of Biscayne Bay, and yachts and other pleasure craft were taking advantage of the late afternoon sunshine. This area, south of Miami, was known for the beauty of its scenery, for the lushness of its vegetation. Palmetto palms and other exotic trees were commonplace here and the richness and colour of plants and flowering shrubs gave the place a decidedly tropical feel.

Coral Gables, she knew, possessed some of the oldest buildings in Miami, and the architecture showed an innately Spanish influence. There were squares and plazas, pools and tumbling fountains. It was also one of the wealthiest parts of the country: Edward's in-laws had taken some pains to impress that upon her, too.

Thinking about Lauren's parents brought her mind back to the reason she was here, and she wished one of them could have come to meet her if their daughter couldn't. They must have known she'd be worried about her brother. Had something happened? Had something gone wrong? Was that why they were bringing her here?

Perhaps he was dead!

The horrifying thought came out of nowhere. It couldn't be true, she told herself fiercely. Dear God, she'd only spoken to him two days ago, and, although he hadn't spared her the details of the car smash that had resulted in him being hos pitalised, at no time had he given her the impression that his condition was critical. He'd been upset, yes; resentful, even. But she'd understood that that was because he still felt like a stranger, hospitalised in a strange country.

Though that was a little ridiculous, too. Technically, Edward was a US citizen. He'd lived in Florida for over three years, and for the last two of those years he'd been married to Lauren Esquival. Well, she'd changed her name to Lauren Leighton when she'd married Edward, of course, Abby corrected herself. Even if it had always been hard to attribute such an Anglo-Saxon surname to her essentially Hispanic sister-in-law.

Abby heaved a sigh.

Something told her this was not going to be an uneventful visit. And, remembering Ross's reaction when she'd told him what she planned to do, going home was not going to be without incident either. Her fiancé—it was still hard to think of him in those terms—had never been one to pull his punches. In his opinion it was high time Edward grew up and started taking responsibility for his own actions, instead of calling on his sister every time he had a problem.

Which wasn't entirely fair, thought Abby a little defensively. All right, when he was younger Edward had been something of a tearaway, and he had relied on his sister to get him out of many of the scrapes he'd got himself into. Nothing too serious, of course. Lots of youths his age had spent money they didn't have. He wasn't a criminal. Nevertheless Abby had spent a goodly portion of her teens and early twenties paying his debts.

Then, when he was nineteen, he'd had what to him had seemed the brilliant idea of going to work in the United States. He'd been studying for a catering diploma at the time, and although Abby had had her doubts when he'd started the course he'd definitely shown an aptitude for the work.

Or perhaps his diligence had been due in part to his infatuation with one of his fellow students, Abby reflected a little cynically now. Whatever, when Selina Steward had taken off for Florida Edward had wasted no time in getting the necessary paperwork and following her.

Abby had been twenty-four then and, although she'd never have admitted as much to Edward, she'd been desolated by his departure. For so long he'd been an integral part of her life. She'd shunned any lasting relationships to be the mother he hardly remembered, and when he'd left she'd had only her career as a teacher to console her.

Still, she'd survived, she conceded ruefully. And she'd been glad when Edward had adapted well to his new surroundings. She'd even convinced herself that it would work out when he'd phoned to say he was going to marry the daughter of the man who owned the Coconut Grove restaurant where he worked. The fact that he and Lauren had only known one another for a matter of months wasn't important, he'd insisted. And, what was more, Abby had to come over for the wedding…

But she was digressing. The wedding and its painful aftermath were long over, and she had to focus on why she was here now. But even the sight of acres of manicured turf—courtesy, so the sign read, of the Alhambra Country Club—and the sunlit plaza that adjoined it couldn't compensate for the feelings of anxiety that were growing inside her. If only she knew what was going on. If only she knew how Edward was, *where* he was…

He had to be all right, she told herself fiercely. She'd never forgive herself if anything had happened to him. All right, as Ross had so painstakingly pointed out, she couldn't hold herself responsible for Edward's decision to move to Florida, and at twenty-two he was surely old enough to look after himself. But Edward would always be her little brother, and Abby supposed it was her own thwarted maternal instinct that made her so protective of him still.

But that was something else she didn't want to get into now. Looking down, she massaged her finger where Ross's diamond sparkled with a cold light. They'd been engaged since Christmas, after knowing one another since before Edward had left for the States. But it was only in recent months that they'd become close.

And now Edward was causing a rift between them. Ross considered her decision to come rushing out here at her brother's behest nothing short of foolhardy. They were planning to get married in six months, for heaven's sake, he'd protested. Wasting money on airfares to Florida, when she had no real proof that her brother was in any danger, was downright stupid.

Well, Ross hadn't exactly said she was stupid. He was far too prudent for that. But he had maintained that after they were married things would be different. She would have to stop behaving as if Edward still needed her to hold his hand.

Abby grimaced. When they were married. Somehow the words had even less conviction here than they'd had back in London. It wasn't that she didn't care for Ross, she told herself. She did. Perhaps she'd just been single too long. Why did she find it so hard to contemplate putting her future in any man's hands?

Or had Alejandro Varga...?

But once again she steered her thoughts away from that disastrous memory. Like her mother's desertion, and her father's subsequent death from alcohol poisoning, it was all water under the bridge now. It had no bearing on the present. She was here to support Edward and nothing else.

Unless Alejandro visited his cousin while she was here.

But that wouldn't happen, she assured herself. His association with Lauren's parents had seemed tenuous at best. As far as she remembered Alejandro was a distant cousin of Mrs Esquival, and his presence in their home had been because of the wedding. Besides, he had a wife. And somehow Abby didn't think he'd want to introduce them.

Her throat tightened in spite of herself, and she was glad that the sudden slowing of the car brought her quickly back to the present. For a few moments she'd been lost in thought, but now she saw that they had entered the residential district where she knew the Esquivals had their estate.

It wasn't an estate such as was meant by the word back in England, of course. The Esquivals' property comprised a rather large villa set in cultivated grounds. There was no parkland surrounding it, no gatehouse. Just a high stone wall protecting it from public view.

The names of the various streets they passed were appealing, and Abby forced herself to look for South Cutler Road, where Lauren's parents lived. Fortunately it was nowhere near Old Okra Road, where Alejandro had his house. She'd have been far more apprehensive if it was.

Abby was just admiring the Renaissance façade of the newly refurbished Gables Hotel when the chauffeur turned his head and spoke to her over his shoulder. 'I guess this is your first visit to Florida, ma'am,' he said, albeit with a heavy Spanish accent, and Abby was so taken aback that for a moment she could only stare at him.

'I—my second,' she got out at last, trying not to feel aggrieved that he'd waited so long before speaking to her. Also, being addressed as 'ma'am' took some getting used to, as well. She touched her hair defensively. Did she really look that old?

'So you've been to the Esquivals' house before?' he went on, and she swallowed.

'Is that where we're going?' she asked, gathering her composure with an effort. 'What about my brother? Do you know how he is?'

'No one told me anything about that, ma'am,' responded the chauffeur annoyingly. 'But as he's staying with the Esquivals right now I guess you'll soon find out.'

Abby's jaw dropped. 'He's staying with the Esquivals?' she echoed disbelievingly. 'But—I understood he was in hospital.'

'Guess he's recovered,' the man remarked laconically. 'Like I say, you'll soon see him for yourself.'

Abby realised she must look as stunned as she felt, and hastily pulled herself together. But all Ross's misgivings were coming home to roost. She should have insisted on speaking to Edward's doctor before she left England. She just hoped her brother hadn't brought her here on a wild-goose chase.

Any further speculation was balked by the realisation that the chauffeur had halted the impressive limousine outside tall electrically operated gates. He barely had time to roll down his window and identify himself to the security cameras before the heavy gates started to open, and they drove up the curving driveway to the Esquivals' sprawling residence.

Not surprisingly now, Abby was anxious, and she found herself moving to the edge of her seat. It was as if she hoped she could precipitate her arrival. For the moment all she could think about was seeing her brother again, and she barely looked at the beautiful Spanish-style house with its ornamental pillars and trailing vines.

The car braked before double-panelled doors, and almost immediately they opened to allow a uniformed maid to run down the shallow steps to meet them. Small and foreign in appearance, she seemed unusually eager to please, opening the door of the limousine, inviting Abby to step out.

'Thanks.'

Abby did so, brushing down the slightly creased legs of her khaki pants. In fact, she was sure she must look distinctly travel-worn, and she wished she'd thought about taking a change of clothes onto the plane.

The khaki pants and cream shirt would have to do, though she thought about taking her jacket out of her haversack. But now that she was out in the sunlight again the heat was almost palpable. She certainly didn't need a jacket. And it was only March.

'Welcome to Miami, *señora*,' the maid greeted her politely as the chauffeur got out to heft Abby's suitcase from the boot. Then, with a distinctly flirtatious air, she added, *'Hola, Carlos. Como esta?'* How are you?

As Abby digested the fact that she now knew the chauffeur's name, he responded to the maid's greeting with rather less enthusiasm. *'Bien, gracias,'* he said, which Abby knew was usually followed by *Y usted?* but wasn't in this case. Then, to Abby, 'I'll leave this here, ma'am.' He put down the heavy case. 'And I hope all goes well with your brother.'

'Oh—thank you.' Abby blinked, wondering if the house was off-limits to the other staff. But when he got back into the limousine and drove away she revised her opinion. She had probably taken him away from his usual work.

To her chagrin, the maid took charge of her case. Lifting the strap, she tugged it on its wheels up the steps, waiting rather impatiently now for Abby to join her.

'Come,' she said, leading the way into the wide entrance hall. It was cooler inside, and a huge urn of flowers spilled scarlet blossoms over the marble surface of a stone table.

Air-conditioning cooled the heat that had beaded on Abby's forehead, and she ran a nervous hand over her hair, feeling the damp strands clinging to her cheeks. She probably looked as flushed and harassed as she felt.

Looking about her, she had to admit she'd forgotten exactly how beautiful the Esquivals' home was. Cool and spacious, it epitomised all that was good about Spanish architecture. Long windows looked out onto an inner courtyard and hanging baskets edged an arching colonnade.

'Mees Leighton—Abigail!' The voice that accosted her was soft and feminine, and Abby turned to find Lauren's mother emerging from the salon that adjoined the reception hall. Small and plump, but exquisitely dressed, Dolores Esquival matched her surroundings, her sleek chignon of dark hair putting Abby's explosion of crinkled red curls to shame. 'Welcome to Florida,' she added, her high heels tapping across the polished floor as she came to meet her guest. Air kisses whispered at either side of Abby's head as she continued, 'I hope you had a good journey, *cara*.'

'I—yes. Thank you.' Abby felt a little bemused as she returned the greeting. Lauren's mother was behaving as if she was here for a holiday instead of flying out to be at her brother's bedside. 'It's very—kind of you to ask.'

'Not so, *querida*.' Was Abby mistaken or did Dolores's mouth tighten a little. 'We are very happy to have you here.'

'Yes, but—'

Ignoring her now, Lauren's mother switched her attention

to the maid, who was hovering in the background, directing her to take their guest's suitcase upstairs. At least that was what Abby thought she was doing. Her imperious signal towards the curving staircase seemed to indicate it was.

'Oh, but—' Abby began, eager to explain that she had no intention of presuming on the Esquivals' hospitality, but Lauren's mother turned to her again.

'This way,' she said, apparently deaf to Abby's protests. 'I am sure you are eager to see your brother,' she added, heading into the salon. 'Everyone is through here.'

Afterwards, when she was unwillingly installed in the first-floor suite she had occupied on her first visit to Florida, Abby marvelled that she had had no suspicion that Alejandro might be there.

Yet how could she have? she asked herself defensively. She'd believed that he was just a distant relative, invited to the wedding because family politics dictated as much. She'd had no idea that he was such a close friend of the Esquivals, nor that Lauren seemed to regard him with a distinctly possessive affection.

Still, when she'd followed Dolores into the enormous salon that seemed to stretch right across the back of the house, she'd had eyes only for her brother. Besides, she'd still been slightly dazzled by the change from sun to shadow. With spots of brilliance dancing before her pupils, she'd been in no condition to instantly register all the people in the room.

Edward was there, she'd seen with some relief, apparently confined to the cushioned divan where he was reclining. With one leg encased in plaster from hip to knee, he had apparently been incapable of coming to greet her. She had hesitated only a moment before hurrying to his side.

'Oh, Eddie,' she exclaimed huskily, suddenly inexplicably near to tears. 'What on earth have you been doing to yourself?'

She bent to kiss his cheek and Edward captured one of her hands and held onto it. 'Hey, Abbs,' he greeted her urgently. Then, in an undertone, 'Thank God you've come!'

Abby's eyes widened at his unexpected words. But before she could say or do anything rash, another hand touched her sleeve.

'Abigail,' declared a vaguely familiar voice. 'How—good it is to see you again.'

Abby turned, straightening, to find Luis Esquival standing right behind her. Lauren's father was only slightly taller than his wife, with a broad dark-skinned face and luxuriant moustaches. He extended his hand towards her. 'Did you have a pleasant journey?'

Abby was confused, as much by her brother's words as by the fairly obvious conclusion that there was nothing seriously wrong with him. He had let her believe that he'd be in hospital for some time, whereas now it appeared that apart from a probable fracture he was okay. Heavens, she thought ruefully, Ross was going to love this.

But Lauren's father was waiting for an answer and, summoning her composure, she managed a polite smile. 'It was— tiring,' she admitted. Plane journeys were not her thing, and she'd had the doubtful privilege of being seated next to the toilets. 'Thank you.'

She glanced round then, expecting to see Lauren, but her sister-in-law wasn't in the room. Instead she saw an elderly woman seated by an arrangement of potted palms, and behind her, standing in the shadows near the ornate brick fireplace was a tall man dressed all in black.

It was strange, but even then she had no inkling that she might know him. So far as she was concerned the only other person she was eager to speak to was Lauren herself. She wanted to find out what was behind Edward's desperate words. She wanted to know why he'd felt the need to send for her.

But once again Luis Esquival demanded her attention. 'We were most surprised when Edward told us you intended paying us a visit,' he said silkily. 'As you can see, your brother is recovering very well.'

Abby was nonplussed. Her eyes sought Edward's, but he was suddenly intensely interested in the cast on his leg. Below the hem of his navy shorts the plaster looked extremely white against his bare skin, and as she watched he shifted a little uneasily in his seat.

'I—I thought—' she was beginning, when the man beside the fireplace suddenly moved into the shaft of sunlight slicing through the half-drawn blinds.

'I am sure—Abigail—was concerned when she heard about her brother's accident,' he drawled in the low, seductively sensual tone that Abby remembered not just in her mind but in her bones. And as she swung round, hardly daring to believe he'd have the nerve to come here and face her, Alejandro Varga acknowledged her dismay with an ironic little smile. 'Abigail.' He inclined his head towards her with all his old arrogance. 'What an unexpected pleasure!'

CHAPTER TWO

You smug bastard!

For a moment Abby was half afraid she'd said the words out loud. But when she glanced apprehensively about her she saw no look of horror on anyone's face, no embarrassed apology trembling on anyone's lips. On the contrary, everyone— excluding Edward—was looking at Alejandro with undisguised approval, and Abby wanted to sink into the floor at the realisation that she was expected to acknowledge him, too.

'Mr Varga,' she said tightly, allowing her eyes to drift only briefly over his dark face. She was sure he must know exactly how she was feeling, and the hot colour that she had never been able to control spread revealingly into her throat.

The fact that she was instantly aware of everything about him, from the sleek smoothness of the hair that brushed his collar at the back of his head to the lean, aristocratic hollows beneath his cheekbones, was irritating. But that was her problem. It would have been difficult to pretend, to herself at least, that his image hadn't been indelibly printed on her memory for the past two years. Just because she hated and despised him it hadn't disappeared. She doubted it ever would.

Narrow arching brows framed eyes so dark she'd once believed they were black. But they weren't. Close inspection had revealed that they were merely dark brown, albeit shadowed by black lashes that any woman would envy.

But that was the only feminine thing about Alejandro Varga. Tall for a man whose appearance proclaimed his Cuban heritage, he had evidently inherited his American mother's genes, too. They were visible in his lean, athletic body, and his long powerful legs. In an impeccably cut suit—Abby guessed it was probably Italian in design—his tie his only concession to col-

16

our, he looked strong and invincible, and so painfully familiar that Abby's heart ached.

God, she had been such a fool, she thought raggedly. It was obvious that as far as he was concerned he had no regrets about the past. And why should he have? To him she had been merely a novelty, a diversion. Edward's older sister, who should have known better than to get involved with a man like him.

Now he was holding out his hand towards her and she was obliged to take it. Anything else would have been taken as an insult to the Esquivals, and she had no quarrel with them.

Nevertheless, when Alejandro's cool fingers closed about hers, she couldn't prevent the shiver that rippled down her spine at his touch. Even in the cool tranquillity of the Esquivals' living room, the memory of those strong brown hands upon her body was unavoidable. Awareness, hot and palpable, spread from his fingers to hers, and whereas before she had been chilled, now she was suddenly engulfed with heat.

Snatching her hand back, she pressed it to her midriff, hoping no one else had noticed her reaction. It would be embarrassing if the Esquivals imagined she was harbouring some abortive feelings for the man. Which she wasn't. But, to divert any suspicion, she added stiffly, 'I didn't expect to see you here.'

'Oh, but Alejandro considers this his second home,' declared Dolores warmly, moving towards him, preventing any rejoinder he might have made. She slipped her hand through his arm. 'Is that not so, *caro*?'

'Thanks to your gracious hospitality,' Alejandro told her gallantly, and Abby, looking away from the tableau they presented, saw her brother's lip curl in undisguised disgust.

No love lost there, then, she reflected curiously, wondering what Edward had against the man. He knew little of her dealings with Alejandro, and as he was apparently a close friend of Edward's in-laws surely it would have been in her brother's interests to try and get along with him. After all, whatever his

faults, there was no doubt that he was a powerful man in
Miami.

But once again she was allowing Alejandro to figure far too
strongly in her thoughts. She hadn't flown several thousand
miles to fret about his relationship with her brother. It was
Edward she was concerned about; Edward whose strange behaviour was definitely a cause for concern.

However, before she could speak to him, she heard the
sound of light footsteps crossing the hall. Everyone glanced
towards the door so that when the young woman whose footsteps they'd heard paused on the threshold, she was instantly
the cynosure of all eyes.

Abby supposed that that was what was meant by making
an entrance. Lauren—for she saw at once that it was her sister-
in-law—gazed about her for a moment before stepping deli-
cately into the room. Small, like her parents, but enviably slen-
der, Lauren was wearing a gauzy floral dress that swished
about her calves. Her ankles looked absurdly narrow above
perilously high-heeled sandals, and Abby was sure she
wouldn't have been able to stand in them, let alone walk.

The younger girl's eyes lingered longest on Alejandro, but
she was too well bred to allow her parents to suspect her smile
of welcome was for anyone other than her sister-in-law. With
a little cry of delight she launched herself towards Abby, enveloping her in a perfumed embrace.

'Abigail,' she exclaimed. 'I did not realise you were already
here.' The slight lisp she favoured added a breathy sibilation
to the words.

Abby managed a warm word of greeting, but she was intensely conscious of the differences between them, and of how
obvious they must appear to everyone else. To Alejandro, she
admitted honestly. He must have noticed she was at least six
inches taller than her sister-in-law, and infinitely more gener-
ously endowed.

Her duty done, Lauren drew back again and turned to smile
at their other guest. 'Alejandro,' she said, and even the way

she said his name was revealing. 'Why did you not let me know you were coming?'

'You mean he didn't?' muttered Edward in an undertone which Abby was fairly sure only she could hear. But her brows drew together in some concern. Surely Edward wasn't jealous of Alejandro Varga. For heaven's sake, the man was married. Though she had to concede that hadn't stopped him before. Even so...

'I did not intend to be here,' Alejandro was saying as Lauren captured his hands and gazed up at him in youthful reproach. 'I had some business I wanted to discuss with your father, that is all. And when I heard that Abigail was expected...' His eyes moved beyond her to where Abby was standing, his brows lifting consideringly. 'How could I leave without first renewing our acquaintance?'

'What a prince!' grunted Edward rudely, but once again only Abby was close enough to hear him. Besides, Dolores was moving forward, eager to make her own contribution.

'Alejandro insisted on sending his chauffeur to the airport to meet Abigail,' she declared, suddenly explaining why Carlos hadn't hung around after dropping her off. And, as Lauren was obliged to relinquish her hold on his hands and turn to her husband, Abby realised that she was now in the ignominious position of being beholden to him, too.

'He's all heart,' said Edward, before she could speak, this time making no attempt to lower his voice. And, although Abby was diverted from having to make a response, she was uncomfortably aware that the Esquivals did not approve of their son-in-law's levity.

'You must forgive Edward,' declared Luis, taking the initiative, his dark eyes hot with anger. 'I fear the accident has not improved his temper, *mi amigo*.' Then, summoning a smile, he turned to Abby again. 'Come, Abigail, let me introduce you to my aunt.'

He drew her across the room to where the elderly woman was sitting. She was nodding in the sunlight that filtered through the long blinds, and he touched her shoulder with a

gentle hand. 'Tia Elena,' he said, his tone softening percepti-
bly, 'do you know Edward's sister? She has come to spend a
few days with us.'

Tia Elena was very old. Her face was a network of lines
and creases, her gnarled hands plucking almost absently at the
embroidery silks in her lap. But her eyes were surprisingly
bright when they opened to Luis's words, her gaze turning up
to Abby's face with undisguised interest

'*Por supuesto,*' she said. Of course. She held out her hand
towards the young woman. 'It is Abigail, *no*?' She paused
'Edward told me you are escaping from the English winter,
si?'

No!

Once again Abby had to bite her tongue to prevent herself
from protesting her innocence. Instead, she shook the old
woman's dry hand and managed a faint smile. 'Who wouldn't
want to escape here?' she said, deciding there was no point in
making an issue of it with the old lady. 'Everything is so—
beautiful.'

'You are saying all the right things,' observed Tia Elena
approvingly. 'Luis, we should hire this young woman to promote your new leisure complex, *no*?'

'You could be right,' responded Luis politely, but Abby had
the impression that he was still finding it difficult to control
his anger. 'Abigail is always welcome here. She knows that

Did she? Abigail was getting the distinct impression that the
Esquivals were not exactly overjoyed that she had arrived
And why not? Edward was obviously in no danger. It looked
very much as if he had got her out here for his own purpose.
But what those purposes were she had yet to find out.

Now Abby abandoned her thoughts and stepped out onto her
balcony. It was good to feel the warmth of the sun reversing
the chill of apprehension on her skin. She already felt like an
interloper and it wasn't pleasant. Particularly as she hadn't
wanted to come.

Yet why did she feel this way? She couldn't fault the

Esquivals' hospitality. Despite Edward's rudeness, a maid had been summoned and iced tea had been served before Abby had been escorted to her room. And, thanks to Tia Elena's attentions, she'd managed to avoid having to say anything to either Alejandro or her brother. She'd perched instead on the edge of a bright yellow sofa and replied to the old lady's questions about her journey.

But why had Edward brought her out here? she wondered restlessly, plucking at the petals of the flowering vine that rioted over the iron railings of the balcony. What possible purpose could he have had? When she'd left England she'd imagined the worst, afraid that there must be something about his injuries he wasn't telling her. Now she was sure there was something Edward hadn't told her—but it wasn't about his accident.

The sound of voices came from below and her scalp prickled. Although she couldn't understand what he was saying, she thought she would have recognised that voice anywhere. It was Alejandro. He was leaving. And all three members of the Esquival family had come out to bid him farewell.

Abby glanced down almost nervously. Her balcony overlooked the formal gardens that lay to the right of the long drive, and by turning her head she could easily see the entrance portico and the four people who had emerged onto the shallow steps.

She knew she should draw back, that even by standing here, watching them, she was invading their privacy, but she stayed where she was. She wished she knew what her sister-in-law was talking about. Lauren's dark excitable posturing intrigued her. It was obvious that they all deferred to the man Abby had never expected to encounter here, and her heart twisted painfully at the way they fawned around him.

Alejandro seemed calm and unruffled. His lazy smile split the dark contours of his face. He gave a polite wave before walking towards the sleek black vehicle that Abby now saw was parked to one side of the forecourt. A click of the key-fob and then he was swinging the door open, coiling his long length behind the wheel.

No wonder the chauffeur hadn't hung around, Abby reflected, reluctantly admiring the lines of the expensive sports saloon. Clearly Alejandro preferred to drive himself.

The Esquivals clustered around the car, reluctant to let him go, but evidently he had had enough. His firing of the ignition signalled his eagerness to be on his way. And, although Abby told herself she was relieved that he would apparently not be joining them for dinner, she couldn't prevent the unexpected frisson of nostalgia she felt as he swung the wheel towards the gates.

Crushing the emotion, she turned and went back into the bedroom behind her. Perhaps she ought to be thinking of leaving, too, she reflected. There was a flight to London tomorrow afternoon at about this time, and if she had any sense she'd arrange to be on it. She owed it to Ross, and to her local education authority, not to take advantage of their good nature. And now that it appeared that all Edward needed was someone to complain to she had no excuse for staying on.

But for tonight at least she had to make the best of the situation. The suite, which comprised this room, a small sitting area, a dressing room and bathroom, was very comfortable. Okay, maybe the rather heavy and ornate furniture was not to her taste, but so what? It suited the house.

Nevertheless, she decided not to take everything out of the case the maid had deposited on the carved chest at the foot of the bed. Fortunately, she'd packed a couple of dresses near the top of the case that she'd hoped would be suitable for both day and evening wear, and that was all she'd need. Oh, and a pair of heels, of course. She couldn't wait to get out of the khaki pants and into something cool and feminine.

Say *what*?

Abby's lips twisted. What was she thinking of? Just because Lauren and her mother chose to wear extremely feminine clothes that was no reason for her to feel she had to do the same. For heaven's sake, she'd always been more at home in jeans and sweaters, or in warmer weather shorts and tees. She was no fashion plate. She never had been. She'd never get away with the kind of fussy flowing outfits Edward's in-laws favoured.

She heaved a sigh. This whole trip was going to be a disaster. She just knew it. She could willingly strangle Edward for getting her into this situation.

A knock at her door brought a momentary halt to her soul-searching. Throwing the two dresses she'd taken from the suitcase onto the bed, she walked resignedly across the sitting area to the door.

Edward was waiting outside. He could evidently get around with the help of the crutches he had propped beneath his arms. He looked a little shamefaced, however, and Abby only hesitated a second before stepping back to let him in.

Closing the door, she leant back against it for a moment. Then, still without saying anything, she walked past him and into the bedroom, returning to the examination of her clothes she'd been making before he'd interrupted her. But her heart wasn't in it, and when her brother limped to stand in the archway, watching her, she was forced to meet his pleading gaze.

'Are you mad at me?' he asked, giving her an appealing look, and she took a calming breath before replying.

'Can you blame me?' she demanded. Then, after a pause, 'You let me think you were seriously injured, Eddie. I was really worried about you. And now I find there's nothing wrong with you that a few weeks' rest won't cure.'

Edward looked injured. 'I wouldn't say that.'

Abby gave him a forbearing look. 'Comparatively speaking,' she retorted shortly. 'What have you got? A fractured femur? Cuts and bruises? Life-threatening? I don't think so.'

Edward limped to the armchair by the open balcony doors and eased himself into it. 'So what are you saying?' he asked. 'That I have to be at death's door before you'd make the effort to come and see me?'

Abby sighed. 'That's not what I meant and you know it.'

'Do I?' Edward was on the offensive now. 'It sounds sus
piciously like it to me.'

'Well, that's because you're choosing to take it that way,
replied Abby, catching on fast. 'And you're not going to make
me feel guilty, Eddie. I know you too well. What's really
going on here? You might as well tell me. I haven't got the
time to waste trying to second-guess you.'

Edward's mouth took on a resentful curve. 'It sounds as i
you don't care what happens to me any more.'

'Oh, Eddie!' Abby flopped down onto the side of the bed
feeling as if she wanted to scream. It was bad enough tha
he'd got her out here in the first place. She could do withou
his self-pity now she was here. 'Stop twisting my words. I'n
pleased to see you again. Of course I am. But you have to
understand, this is not a holiday for me.'

'It's not a holiday for me either,' muttered Edward pee
vishly, and Abby shook her head.

'You know what I mean. I've had to take leave of absenc
from school, and now that Ross and I are—'

'Oh, I wondered when Kenyon would come into it,' Edward
interrupted her harshly, and Abby remembered belatedly tha
he didn't care for Ross any more than her fiancé cared fo
him.

They'd all met last year, when Edward had brought Laure
to see where he'd used to live in England, and Abby recalle
how she'd hoped that the two men would hit it off. Her re
lationship with Ross had still been in its initial stages at tha
time, and it had seemed a good idea to get the two men to
gether.

It hadn't worked. Ross had considered Edward selfish an
immature, and her brother had resented the occasionally pa
tronising attitude Ross had adopted. She'd tried to explain tha
Ross was used to dealing with recalcitrant teenagers, but tha
had only exacerbated the situation. Edward had accused he
of implying that he was no better than one of Ross's student
and in her efforts to placate him she'd inadvertently offende

Ross, too. The whole affair had been a nightmare, and she should have known better than to mention her fiancé now.

However, before she could think of some way of defusing the situation, Edward spoke again. Scuffing the toe of his canvas shoe against the polished floor, he lifted one shoulder in a conciliatory gesture.

'Anyway,' he mumbled, barely audibly, 'you're right. I didn't ask you to come out here just because of the accident.'

Abby's brows, which were considerably darker than her hair, drew rather warily together. 'You didn't?' she asked carefully, as if she hadn't been implying as much for the past few minutes. 'So why did you ask me to come?'

Edward blew out a breath. 'I—well, I needed to talk to you about Lauren. I think she's having an affair.'

CHAPTER THREE

ABBY was stunned. 'You're not serious!'

'Why not?' Edward, who had been staring moodily at the rug he had displaced with his toe, now looked up. 'Don't you think any man would want to have an affair with her?'

'Don't be silly.' Sometimes Abby was inclined to agree with Ross's assessment of the younger man. 'That has nothing to do with it.' She hesitated. 'What I mean is, I can't imagine why you would think such a thing.'

Or could she? Unwillingly Abby remembered how Lauren had behaved towards Alejandro Varga. Even if their relationship allowed for some familiarity, Abby had noticed that she'd been inordinately pleased to see him.

Edward scowled now, his next words shocking her out of any lingering sense of complacency. 'What am I supposed to think when she takes every chance she gets to spend time with Varga?' he demanded. 'And now that I'm half crippled with this leg, I don't even know where she is half the time.'

Abby's jaw had dropped as he spoke, but now she hurriedly rescued it. 'You're not implying she's having an affair with—with Alejandro?' she exclaimed disbelievingly.

'Why not?' Edward's pale eyes challenged hers.

'Well, because—because he's married?'

'Not any more.'

'Not any more?' Abby blinked. 'You mean, he's—divorced?'

'It happens,' said Edward bitterly. 'I always knew Maria was too good for him.'

Abby didn't know what to say. The last thing she wanted was for Edward to imagine she was still interested in Alejandro. All the same...

26

'Are you saying that Lauren had something to do with him getting a divorce?' she ventured incredulously, and Edward hunched his shoulders.

'No.' He was impatient. 'That happened a while ago. He and Maria were having problems before we even got married.'

'They were?'

Abby tried to hide her reaction from him. She clearly remembered Edward giving her the impression that Alejandro. and his wife were happy together. That Dolores had been devastated when Maria had suffered a family emergency and hadn't been able to attend the wedding.

What emergency had that been? Her impending divorce?

Aware that Edward was watching her rather suspiciously, Abby realised that her face was far too expressive. Raising defensive eyebrows at him, she opted for a casual enquiry. 'What?'

'You tell me,' he said. 'Why are you looking at me like that?'

'Like what?'

'Don't pretend you don't know.' Edward was resentful now. 'I bet you were thinking that that wasn't what I said before.'

Abby chose to be obtuse. '*What* wasn't what you said before?' she asked, refusing to make it easy for him.

'That Varga and his wife were having problems,' he retorted. 'Okay, I admit it. I wanted to put you off him. I could see you were attracted to him, and I didn't want someone like him involved with my sister.'

Abby stared at him. 'So, what are you saying? That you told lies about him?'

'Not lies, no.' Edward was defensive. 'I just exaggerated the truth a little, that's all. No big deal.'

Abby shook her head in disbelief. 'And what gave you the right to interfere in my life?'

'Oh, let's not get carried away here,' protested Edward insensitively. 'The chances of you and Varga getting it together weren't exactly likely, were they? I mean, I know you were flattered when he offered to take you sightseeing and all, but you have to understand that's what these guys are like. Coming on to a woman—any woman—is second nature to them, and Varga more than most. I never liked him. I hoped that when the wedding was over he'd crawl back under his stone.' He scoffed. 'Some chance!'

'Edward!'

'Well…' He was unrepentant. 'I assumed he was just a distant relative. I had no idea he'd become such a constant presence in our lives. Do you know, he's a major shareholder in Luis's company? This new leisure complex they're hoping to open next Christmas is being financed by Varga. He and Luis are partners. Partners! How do you think that makes me feel? I'm Luis's son-in-law, not Alejandro.'

Abby was stunned—as much by the fact that Edward had lied to her as by his obvious envy of the other man. She didn't know what she thought of his suspicions about Alejandro and Lauren. She would reserve judgement. But after what he'd told her, how dependable was anything he said?

She was so glad now that she'd never confided her own feelings to Edward. Though perhaps it would have been easier if she had. Surely then he would have thought twice about involving her in his present problems. Yet, knowing Edward as she did there were no guarantees.

Feeling her way, she said cautiously, 'I still don't see what you're saying. All right. I accept that—that Alejandro is a regular visitor to the house. But you and Lauren don't live here. You have your own apartment, don't you? In Coconut Grove.'

Edward gave her an exasperated look. 'You don't know much about Cuban families, do you?' he snorted. 'Well, let me tell you, they stick together. Like, living in each other's pockets, if you know what I mean? Sure, we have our own place, but Lauren's hardly ever there. When I'm at work she's more often here. Or somewhere else, if you get my drift?'

'Somewhere else?' Abby suspected she knew what he was getting at but she decided to let him go on.

'Yeah.' Edward scowled. 'Making nice with—Alejandro.'

He pronounced the other man's name just as Lauren did, and Abby's stomach tightened unpleasantly. 'But he's her cousin,' she protested. 'Cousins don't get involved with one another in this country. I read it somewhere. It's considered too close a relationship.'

'Tell that to my wife,' retorted Edward dourly. 'In any case, he's not her cousin. Not exactly. He's a distant relation of her mother's.'

Abby sighed. 'Even so—'

'Even so, I know what I'm talking about,' snapped Edward irritably. 'I might have known you wouldn't believe me. It's Kenyon, isn't it? He's poisoned your mind against me.'

'Don't be so ridiculous!' Abby gasped. 'Ross couldn't do such a thing. I just—' She paused. 'What proof do you have?'

'What more proof do I need? You saw them together. Can you honestly tell me that you didn't think they seemed pretty close for distant cousins?'

Abby pushed herself up from the bed, feeling incredibly weary suddenly. It had been a long day. It might only be early evening in Miami, but it was after eleven o'clock back home. And, after all the upheaval, she'd forgotten to phone her fiancé as she'd promised. Would he understand that she'd had other things on her mind?

But breaking a promise to Ross was the least of her worries, she thought heavily. When she'd agreed to come here she'd hoped to avoid any mention of the man who'd caused such anguish in her life. Now it seemed he was an integral part of Edward's reasons for contacting her. And she so much didn't want to have to think about Alejandro again.

She'd done all her thinking and regretting two years ago, she thought bitterly. Even if, as it appeared now, he hadn't been as black as she'd painted him in her own mind. But he'd still behaved quite heartlessly. She didn't think she'd ever forgive him for that.

'Abbs?'

Edward was gazing up at her with a look of hopeful expectation on his face and she guessed he wasn't thinking about her. Had it ever occurred to him that she might have a life of her own? she wondered. As far as Edward was concerned, she'd only ever been there for him.

'I'm tired,' she told him now, glancing longingly towards the large colonial bed. But as that evidently wasn't the right answer, judging by his sulky face, she tried again. 'I just don't know what you want from me, Eddie. I'm only going to be here for a couple of days. If you're expecting me to spy on your wife for you, then—'

'Hey, I didn't ask you here to act like some kind of private eye,' exclaimed Edward impatiently. 'I doubt if you'd be any good at it anyway.' He grimaced. You're not exactly the inconspicuous type!'

Abby caught her breath. 'You know,' she said tensely, 'I've a good mind to phone the airport here and now and ask how soon I can get a flight home. I realise you're upset about Lauren, but that doesn't give you the right to insult me.'

'I'm not insulting you,' Edward snorted angrily 'Dammit, you couldn't be further from the truth. Okay, maybe I'm no good at choosing the right words. I'm not an English graduate, am I?' he taunted. 'What I'm trying to say is, people notice you. Hell, they'd notice any tall redhead around here. You may have noticed. They're not exactly thick on the ground.'

Abby expelled a resigned breath. 'If you say so.'

'I do say so.' Edward tried to reach out and grasp her hand but she evaded him. 'Come on, Abbs. Lighten up. You could at least say it's good to see me again.'

Abby shook her head. 'I'd just like to know why you've brought me here,' she said. 'I mean, I am glad to see you again, but if it's just my advice you want you could have had that over the phone.'

Edward's hand dropped onto his thigh. 'Well, that's telling me straight, isn't it?'

'Eddie!'

'Oh, all right.' He levered himself up from the chair and, using the crutches, made his way out onto the balcony. 'I want your help.'

'My help?' Abby followed him to the doorway, watching as he turned and propped his back against the railings. 'How am I supposed to help you? Do you want to come back to England? Is that it? Do you need my support to get started again over there?'

'As if!' Edward looked incredulous now. 'Abby, nothing could persuade me to come back to England again. I like it here. It's my home. Not this house, of course, although with a bit of luck it will be mine one day.' He grinned momentarily, and then, realising his sister was watching him with appalled eyes, he sobered. 'No, what I mean is, I've got a good job at the restaurant. I'd be a fool to even think about leaving Florida and starting again.'

'Then—?'

'Give me time,' he protested. 'I'm getting there. But this isn't easy for me, Abbs. I don't want you to think I haven't thought this through.'

'Thought what through?' Abby could feel herself getting edgy. 'Eddie, if you expect me to try and persuade Lauren—'

'Lauren?' He pushed himself away from the railings and came back to where she was standing. 'Lauren wouldn't listen to anything you had to say.' He pulled a face. 'She's blind and deaf to any criticism where Varga is concerned.'

'Well, that's good, because I was going to say I wouldn't do it,' retorted Abby shortly. 'Come on, Eddie, get to the point.'

Edward hung his head, staring down at the plaster that encased his leg as if he hoped it would provide him with some inspiration. Then, when she was on the point of yelling at him, he said, 'As a matter of fact I don't want to you to *talk* to anyone.' He paused. 'I want you to use any means necessary to get Varga off my back.'

It was barely light when Abby opened her eyes. Her body clock was still working on British time, and even though she'd found it incredibly difficult to get to sleep the night before, she had no desire to stay in bed now.

Being tired didn't stop her brain from working. It just added to the chaos in her head. She couldn't wait to escape the turmoil of uncertainty that was gripping her. Dear God, what was she going to do?

Although it was almost twelve hours since Edward had exploded his bombshell, she still felt numb. No, that wasn't true. If she'd still felt numb she wouldn't be suffering such a sense of betrayal. Wouldn't be wondering if she'd ever trust her brother again.

Had he actually asked her to try and use her influence on Alejandro? Did he really believe that the other man would care about anything she had to say? It was two years since she'd spoken to the Cuban; two years and many hours of heartache she couldn't bear to go through again.

Besides, speaking to Alejandro was only a part of what he wanted. As Edward had implied when he was talking about his wife, words wouldn't accomplish anything at all. What he really needed was for her to try and rekindle whatever interest Alejandro had had in her. He was asking her to jerk Alejandro's chain. To do whatever was necessary to distract the other man's attentions from his wife.

In other words to seduce him, if she could.

And what kind of a brother would ask his sister to do something like that?

Throwing back the covers, Abby thrust her feet out of bed. She had the distinct feeling she was dreaming all this. But when she accidentally stood on an earring that she'd dropped the night before, and it dug into the pad of her foot, she realised it was no dream.

A nightmare, maybe, she thought, bending to pick up the circle of gold and automatically threading it through her ear. Certainly last night's dinner hadn't been exactly what she'd expected, and it had been apparent from the Esquivals' behaviour that they thought she'd invited herself here.

'How long can you stay?' Dolores had asked politely, passing her a bowl of rice and beans so that she could serve herself. 'Edward couldn't tell us what your plans were.'

I bet he couldn't, Abby had fumed silently, noticing that once again Edward was avoiding her eyes. But, 'I'm not sure,' she'd responded, deciding he shouldn't have it all his own way. 'When Edward told me about his accident I felt I ought to come and see how he was for myself. I hope you don't mind.'

'Of course we don't mind,' Luis Esquival had assured her smoothly, his innate courtesy not allowing him to make any other response. 'You are Edward's sister, Abigail. You are welcome here at any time. I hope your brother assured you of that.'

Abby had managed a smile, but she felt uneasy at accepting their hospitality under false pretences. She'd hardly been able to swallow any of the rather spicy rice and fried beef, which Dolores had told her was a Cuban speciality, and when the meal was over she'd pleaded tiredness and retired to her room.

She'd hardly exchanged two words with her sister-in-law all evening. Lauren had seemed singularly reticent to get involved in what little conversation there was, and Abby wondered if she suspected why she was here. Surely not. Edward wouldn't have told her. Though in retrospect Abby had to admit that Lauren had said very little to her husband either.

So what was she to gauge from that? Did Edward have some justification for his suspicions? He'd left her in no doubt that he believed his happiness was at stake. He'd even told her that he didn't know how he would go on if Lauren left him. And, while Abby was sure that was an exaggeration, nothing could alter the fact that he was distraught.

She shook her head. The whole situation was unbelievable. Could he really have invited her here because of some fleeting interest he thought Alejandro had shown in her two years ago? How was she supposed to get a man who was virtually a stranger to her, despite their torrid history, to choose her company over that of his cousin? It was ludicrous. She was engaged to Ross, for heaven's sake. Just because Edward didn't like him that didn't mean she could ignore her fiancé's feelings and act like a—a tart!

Picking up the matching earring from the table beside the bed, she padded across the floor to the windows, securing it to her ear as she went. Then, drawing the blinds aside, she unlatched the balcony doors and stepped out into the comparative coolness of early morning.

A sliver of brightness on the horizon heralded the imminent arrival of the sun, but for the moment the garden below was shrouded in shadow. Yet already she could hear the sound of running water and guessed someone was tending to the plants. The lawns didn't get to be so green by accident, she mused, and, unwilling to be observed in just her nightshirt, she turned and went back into her room.

Deciding a shower would serve the dual purpose of filling time and helping to clear her head, Abby walked into the bathroom. It was such a treat, she thought wryly. When she stayed at Ross's house she had to compete with him for the shower, and her fiancé tended to ignore the fact that the hot water wasn't unlimited. He often left it running needlessly, so that when Abby went for her shower the water was cold.

She didn't have that problem this morning. But it did remind her that she had to ring Ross before she did anything else. Knowing him, she was sure he'd have checked that her flight had arrived safely, but she still needed to explain what was going on.

Or not.

Heaving a sigh, she adjusted the shower, wondering what on earth she was going to tell her fiancé when she made her call. If she told him that Edward wasn't seriously hurt he'd expect her to return home almost immediately. And that was what she should do, she chided herself fiercely. If she just pretended that she'd made a mistake Ross need never know what Edward had asked of her.

Stepping into the pulsating stream of water, she wondered why she was even hesitating. Delaying her return was just giving her brother false hope. All right, she was prepared to accept that he and Lauren might be going through a bad patch. These things happened. But nothing she did was going to change things. It was up to him to make an effort, to do everything in his power to rekindle whatever it was that had attracted her to him in the first place.

There were bottles of shower gel and shampoo on a glass shelf to one side of the shower, and Abby chose a lemon-scented mousse to wash her hair. It was good to massage her scalp, to feel the cleansing fragrance refreshing her completely. She emerged feeling infinitely brighter, if no less certain of what she was going to do.

The long mirrors that lined the walls of the bathroom were barely steamed when she stepped out. Reaching for a towel from the rack, she dried herself quickly and then used the towel to rub the condensation from the mirror nearest to her. Surveying her appearance with a critical eye, she wondered why on earth Edward thought that Alejandro might prefer her to Lauren. It just wasn't realistic, however she might feel about it.

She shook her head and the tumbled tangle of dark red curls sprayed water all over her dry shoulders. Reaching for the towel, she dabbed herself dry again, aware as she did so that her nipples were suddenly tight and hard. It was because she'd shivered, she assured herself, turning away from the mirror. But not before her eyes had made a swift appraisal of her narrow waist and rounded hips.

The realisation that what she was really doing was trying to see herself with Alejandro's eyes irritated her. Did she really care what he thought of her now? Or was she naïve enough to believe Edward's assessment of her appearance? A final glance at her backside convinced her. Her brother was desperate, and he'd say anything to get his own way.

CHAPTER FOUR

SHE decided to ring Ross before drying her hair.

With the balcony doors open, heat was spreading into the room from outside, and she turned the thermostat down to warm the room. Then, wrapping the folds of the towelling robe she had found behind the bathroom door more closely about her, she seated herself in the chair Edward had used the night before and picked up the phone.

Discovering she had an outside line, she dialled the school where they were both employed. It was still early, but Ross should be taking his lunch at this time. One of the school secretaries put her through to the staff room and she was relieved when Ross himself answered the call.

'Abby!' he exclaimed, after she'd identified herself. 'I thought you were going to ring me last night. I waited up until after midnight, hoping you wouldn't forget.'

'I know. I'm sorry.' Abby wished he hadn't had to begin with a complaint. 'And I didn't forget. Not exactly. It's just—well, I'm staying with Eddie's in-laws at the moment, and it's a little—complicated.'

'What's a little complicated? Your brother's injuries?' Ross immediately leapt to the wrong conclusion and Abby sighed.

'No,' she said, knowing that he deserved a straight answer. 'Eddie's injuries aren't complicated, but—'

'But it's going to take more than a couple of days to get him home again, is that it?'

Ross's attempts to second-guess her were annoying and Abby wished he'd just listen to what she had to say instead of jumping in every few seconds with his own version of events.

'I—Eddie's out of hospital,' she persisted, trying to explain

36

that he was staying with the Esquivals, too. But Ross seemed determined to put his own interpretation on her words.

'Oh, I see,' he said, when he obviously didn't see at all. 'He's back at the flat. I suppose Lauren's looking after him. But that's only a small place, isn't it? Is that why you're staying with her parents?'

Abby blew out an exasperated breath. 'No,' she said shortly. 'Neither of them are at the—apartment.' She deliberately used the alternative term. 'They're staying here.'

'They are?' For the first time her fiancé sounded less sure of himself. Then, almost as an afterthought, 'So, how is Edward? Have you found out what happened?'

'I know what happened,' said Abby, trying not to be impatient. 'A drunk driver slammed into his car. He was lucky he was hit on the nearside and that he wasn't carrying any passengers. He could have been killed.'

'Well, he evidently wasn't very badly hurt if they've discharged him from hospital already,' said Ross practically. 'I thought as much. So when are you coming home?'

Until that moment Abby had been thinking about going home. She'd all but abandoned any thought of taking what Edward had said seriously, and, although she was worried about the problems he and Lauren were having, she'd had no intention of interfering in their lives.

But Ross's casual assumption that if Edward wasn't in any danger she'd be catching the next flight back to London caught her on the raw. He might show some concern for the man he was planning to make his brother-in-law. His annoying habit of always having to be right infuriated her.

'I don't know,' she said now, deciding it served him right for being so unfeeling. 'I may stay on for a few days.'

'But why?' Ross seemed insensible to the fact that he was treading on dangerous ground. 'Surely he doesn't need you to hold his hand. He's got a wife, Abby. I doubt if she appreciates you turning up out of the blue.'

'I didn't come here because of Lauren,' retorted his fiancée tersely. 'You don't seem to realise the emotional stress an accident can cause.'

But as she said the words Abby wondered who she was kidding. For heaven's sake, if Edward was stressed it wasn't because of the accident. She knew that.

'Oh, right.' Ross sounded irritated now. 'I'd forgotten what a sensitive flower Edward is.' He made a sound of derision. 'Get real, Abby. Edward doesn't need you. He's just using this to get back at me. I bet it really ticked him off when you told him we were engaged.'

'Is that what you really think?' Abby was appalled at his hostility. 'For heaven's sake, Ross, I didn't ring you to get a lecture about my brother's character. He's had a bad shock, okay? Is it any wonder if he needs some moral support?'

'Moral support!' Ross snorted. 'Sometimes I wonder about you, I really do. You're so easily duped. No wonder Edward can run rings around you. Well, after we're married things are going to change. I'm going to let him know he can't come running to you every time he needs a shoulder to cry on.'

Abby caught her breath. 'We may not be getting married at this rate,' she said, wishing she'd never made this call. 'I've got to go, Ross. I'll speak to you later.'

'Well, where—?'

But Abby didn't wait to hear any more. With a feeling of revulsion she put down the phone, staring at it blindly for a few seconds before getting up and moving away. She was glad he couldn't call her back, she thought tensely. Although he knew Edward's number, he didn't know this one. He could be so unpleasant at times. He hadn't even asked her about her journey. He didn't seem to care about anything except when she was going back.

Surely he should sense how she was feeling. Why couldn't he have been sympathetic, understanding? If he had been, she'd probably have been packing her bags right now. As it was, she'd committed herself to staying on for several more days when she hadn't intended to. Either that or run the risk of Ross believing he'd got his own way again.

A glance at her watch reminded her that it was almost eight o'clock. She didn't know where, or even if, the Esquivals had breakfast, but she was desperate now to get out of her room. She'd go downstairs, she decided. Maybe Lauren would join her. She'd welcome the chance to speak to the other girl. Anything was better than staying here at the mercy of her thoughts.

It was already hot. She could feel the heat pouring into the room from outside now, and after closing the balcony doors she turned the air-conditioning up again. Immediately a draught of deliciously cool air swept over her shoulders as she shed the robe and rummaged in her suitcase for something to wear.

By the time she'd found a sleeveless shirt and denim shorts her hair was practically dry. But it was unruly, and snatching up her brush, she quickly plaited the damp curling strands into a single braid. It wasn't very long. It barely reached to the top of her shoulderblades. But at least it was tidy, even if a few wispy curls persisted in escaping to cling to her flushed cheeks.

She didn't bother with make-up. In this heat it wouldn't last, and her face was glowing as it was. Probably due to her rising temperature, she reflected. Unlike many redheads, she did tan, so her skin still retained some of the colour she'd acquired in southern Italy the summer before. Perhaps no one would notice, she hoped optimistically. At least she didn't look as anaemic as she felt.

Her legs looked very pale, though, she conceded, as she went out onto the gallery that circled the hall below. But it was still winter back home and she wasn't used to exposing them. Nevertheless, they were long and slim, even if Edward was fooling himself if he thought any man would notice her while his wife was around.

There was no one about when she reached the ground floor, and after getting her bearings she walked along the wide passageway that led to the back of the house. A sunlit terrace, enclosed by long screens, gave access to an inner courtyard, and the mingled scents of a dozen exotic blooms assaulted her senses.

Stepping out of the shadows of a colonnade that ran along two sides of the courtyard, Abby saw the glinting waters of the swimming pool ahead of her. She wondered if anyone used it these days. When she'd been here two years ago none of the Esquivals had ever been tempted to swim in its lucid depths. As far as they were concerned it was an ornament, a status symbol. As necessary to their lives as the gymnasium in the basement which no one used either.

Pushing her hands into the pockets of her shorts, Abby walked down the two shallow steps that divided the pool deck from the courtyard above. She wasn't thinking about anything at that moment except how delightful it would be to have the freedom to immerse herself in the cool water, and she was shocked when a tall, dark-clad figure rose up from beside the pool.

It was Alejandro. Wearing a black tee shirt and black trousers, he had evidently been sitting on one of the shaded loungers that stood in a regimented row beneath a hedge of flowering bougainvillaea. Lean and imposing, he was looking at her with dark enigmatic eyes, and Abby's mouth dried at the realisation that she didn't know what she was going to say to him.

'Abigail,' he greeted her, inclining his head politely. 'I am sorry if I startled you. I thought perhaps you had seen me.'

And come down here to speak to you? contributed Abby silently. As if she would! The truth was, if she'd seen him first she'd probably have turned tail and gone back into the house.

And how mature was that?

'I—no,' she answered now, glancing back over her shoulder, hoping for deliverance. 'You're an early caller. Are you waiting for Luis?'

'No.' Alejandro's mouth compressed for a moment. 'As a matter of fact, none of the family knows I am here. Except for yourself, *por supuesto*.' He paused. 'Does that bother you?'

'Why should it bother me?' she retorted, stung for a moment into revealing her true feelings. But then, realising that was hardly the image Edward would want her to promote, she added, 'Not at all.'

'Good.' Alejandro turned and indicated the row of loungers behind him. 'Perhaps you will join me?'

Abby saw now that there was a tray residing on the glass-topped table beside the chair he had been occupying. A jug of freshly squeezed orange juice and two glasses, a pot of coffee, and two cups. He had evidently been expecting company, whatever he said, and she wondered with a momentary frisson of distaste if Lauren had stood him up.

But, no. That was pandering to Edward's paranoia, and she had no reason to assume the worst. One of the maids had made an error, had provided breakfast for two instead of one.

'I'm—not sure that would be a good idea,' she said at last, even if this was an opportunity to find out what she wanted to know. 'I was looking for Lauren. Do you know if she's about?'

'If I know my cousin, she is unlikely to appear much before noon,' Alejandro said smoothly. 'I am sorry I cannot help you there. Perhaps you will reconsider my invitation instead.'

He had taken a step towards her and Abby had to steel herself not to retreat before his potent masculinity. Her skin prickled in anticipation of his touch, however, and although she might deny it to herself he could still set her pulses racing just by standing close to her.

'I—don't know,' she said unevenly, wishing she could put her emotions aside and deal with him as casually as he was dealing with her. What was wrong with her, for heaven's sake? It wasn't as if she still believed in hearts and flowers, after all. After her brief encounter with this man she'd been very careful not to trust too much again.

'I do not think there would be any harm in us sharing a pot of coffee,' Alejandro said now, and for a moment she thought he was going to take her arm and guide her to a chair. 'Do not be alarmed, Abigail. I only wish to speak with you. That is all.'

Was she supposed to be grateful for that? Abigail wondered what he was really thinking behind that cool, disturbing mask. 'Well—all right,' she submitted at last, a little breathily. If she wanted him to believe she'd forgotten what had happened two years ago, she would have to do better than this. 'Where do you want me to sit?'

Alejandro drew back to indicate a chair at right angles to the table. 'I think you would be most comfortable there, in the shade,' he replied, and she sucked in her breath as she circled round him, desperate to avoid any contact between them. He waited until she was seated before taking the chair opposite, sitting sideways on the recliner, legs spread to accommodate the table. 'Which would you prefer? Orange juice or coffee?'

In actual fact, Abby would have preferred orange juice, but she needed the caffeine so she chose coffee instead. To her surprise, Alejandro lifted the pot himself, asking her preference for milk and sugar before passing a cup to her.

She was tempted to say *Isn't this cosy?* but she restrained herself. It was just the bubble of hysteria in her stomach that was putting such ideas into her head. Still, the thought of her sitting here, drinking coffee with the man who had seduced her after her brother's wedding and then allowed her to return to England without once attempting to find out if she was all right was quite incredible. Did he have no shame? When was he going to mention that he'd forgotten to tell her that he had had a wife?

But that was all in the past, she reminded herself. Concentrating on the swirling coffee in her cup, she forced herself to put such memories aside. What she ought to be asking herself was why he'd invited her to join him. Why would he want to spend any time with her? The fleeting attraction he'd felt for her was dead and buried. She was right to be suspicious about his motives now.

Nevertheless, she remembered unwillingly, he had wanted

her once. Had wanted to have sex with her, at least. Well, he'd achieved his aim, she thought, an angry sob rising in her throat. So what now? A belated apology for past sins? Her lips twisted. More likely a plea that she wouldn't spoil his current plans by denouncing him to his family.

She noticed that although Alejandro had poured himself a cup of strong black coffee he didn't touch it. Instead, he played with the gold signet ring on his smallest finger, causing it to glint hypnotically in the sunlight. His hands hung between his thighs and Abby had to force herself not to watch him—had to force her eyes not be to be drawn to the taut seam of his pants between his legs.

'You are looking good, Abigail,' he said abruptly, and she set her cup down in its saucer rather harder than she'd intended. This was not what she'd expected at all. 'How are you? I understand you are still teaching. You are quite happy to pursue your career?'

'I have to earn a living, if that's what you mean,' she responded tersely, wondering why he'd be interested enough to find out, and Alejandro inclined his head.

'*Por supuesto*. Of course.' A half-smile touched his lips. 'Edward would have told me if your circumstances had changed.'

Would he? Abby doubted that very much. Why would Edward tell him anything? What he meant was that Edward would have mentioned it to his in-laws and it might then have found its way to his ears.

'Do you see much of Edward?' she asked, deciding this was as good a way as any of finding out what Alejandro thought of her brother, and the dark man gave her a level look.

'Did he not tell you?' he countered surprisingly, and once again she gave him a wary look.

'I—I believe you and—and Luis are working together these days,' she said obliquely, reminding herself to keep her tone impartial. 'Do you—er—do you spend a lot of time here?'

Alejandro studied her expression for a moment, before responding drily, 'Is that a polite way of finding out if I am likely to be—what is it you say?—under your feet?'

'No!' Abby's face was suddenly suffused with hot colour. 'What you do is nothing to do with me, Mr Varga. I was just wondering why—why you are here so early, that's all.'

'And I thought I had made that clear.' Alejandro arched a dark brow. 'And—*Mr* Varga? Do you honestly think we can behave as if there was never anything between us?'

Oh, God!

Abby had been about to pick up her coffee cup again, but now she pressed her hands together in her lap. She'd never dreamt that he might confront her with what had happened two years ago. Had he no shame? Or did he just enjoy making her squirm?

'I'd prefer not to talk about it,' she said at last, though she balked at addressing him as *Mr* Varga again. She didn't want to anger him. That would be foolish. 'It was a mistake I'd just as soon forget.'

Alejandro's mouth compressed. 'You think?' he said, regarding her flushed face for several long nerve-racking seconds. His eyes dropped to the ring on her finger. 'Edward told me there was a new man in your life.'

A new man?

Abby didn't know what he meant by that, but she had no intention of entering into a discussion about her private life. It was hard enough to believe Edward would have told him anything. And that rekindled all the suspicions about Lauren her brother had raised.

'Look,' she said, trying not to sound concerned, 'what is this all about? And please don't tell me you're interested in what I've been doing. It's a little late to find your conscience now.'

'My conscience?' He seemed amazed by her directness. 'I am sure your brother has told you I do not have such a thing. But you, Abigail—you are different from Edward. And I still find you attractive. Please have no doubts about that.'

Abby was stunned into silence. Had he guessed why

Edward had tricked her into coming here? But, if so, did that mean there was some truth in what Edward had been saying? Were he and Lauren really involved in an affair?

'I—my brother has had an accident,' she said unevenly. 'That's the only reason why I'm here.'

'If you say so,' he said, his eyes dark and guarded. 'But your brother has another agenda, I think.'

Abby swallowed. 'I don't know what you mean,' she said, not sure now she even wanted to know.

'Edward has a hairline fracture to his leg,' he said, his tone dismissive. 'Hardly life-threatening, I think you will agree.'

The fact that Abby herself had said much the same when she'd found out was not an issue. 'He's had a terrible shock,' she insisted tensely. 'He could have been killed—'

'But he was not,' inserted Alejandro unfeelingly, much like her fiancé. 'Forgive me, Abigail, but your brother leads far too charmed a life to have it taken away by a drunken driver. The accident was unfortunate, but not serious. The car was damaged, *sí*, but it was not a write-off.'

Abby pushed back her chair and got to her feet. Whatever Edward expected of her, she couldn't stand any more of this. Did Alejandro know why Edward had brought her here, or was he only guessing? And why, when he insisted he was still interested in her, did she feel so aggrieved when this was exactly what her brother had hoped?

'If you'll excuse me…' she said, not really caring whether he did or not. But Alejandro wasn't finished with her.

When she would have circled the table and hurried up the steps to the terrace, he moved into her path. 'You are not leaving already,' he said, and although it was said innocently enough Abby thought it sounded like a warning. 'We have not finished our discussion, Abigail. Edward is not going to like it if you don't get a favourable result.'

'How dare you?'

Abby was so incensed her hand moved automatically towards his face. But Alejandro's hand was quicker, trapping her wrist in mid-flight, holding it effortlessly away from harm.

'I think not,' he said softly, his warm breath lifting the unruly strands of hair from her cheek. 'If your brother wants my help, you will have to do better than this, *cara*. I regret the need to use these methods, Abigail, but I did not make the rules.'

CHAPTER FIVE

LOOKING back, Abby didn't quite know how she'd managed to get away from Alejandro with her dignity still intact.

Her first impulse had been to drag her wrist out of his grasp and run, kicking and screaming her frustration, into the house.

Not, she acknowledged later, that she'd have got away from him without his co-operation. Whatever else, Alejandro was infinitely stronger than she was, and indulging in a childish tug-of-war, with her arm as the rope, would have been downright stupid.

Not to mention embarrassing.

And painful.

But, with her lungs constricting in her chest and her panic only lightly controlled, she'd found the guts to stand up to him. And when it had become apparent that she wasn't going to answer him Alejandro had opened his fingers and released her.

It wasn't over. She knew that. Even though he'd let her go without another word, she knew it as surely as if he'd voiced his desire for retribution. Something was going on here, something she knew nothing about, and she couldn't wait to speak to Edward and find out what the hell it was.

In that, however, she had not been successful. Whether her brother knew of her encounter with Alejandro that morning or not, she didn't know, but he had proved suspiciously elusive since then.

Abby, herself, would have preferred to spend the rest of the morning in her room. But, after sluicing her hot face in the basin in her bathroom, she'd known that would achieve nothing. Even if Alejandro joined the family for breakfast she had to show her face. Besides, how else was she going to corner her brother when she had no idea where his suite of rooms was?

In any case, she could hardly confront her brother in front of his wife. According to Edward, it was because of Lauren that he'd brought her here. And, although she suspected there was more to it than that, she couldn't dismiss his fears out of hand. Alejandro had virtually admitted that something was going on. But she had no idea what it was.

She had breakfast alone.

When she eventually summoned up the courage to go downstairs again, it was to find that no one else was about. The maid directed her to a rattan table and chairs set in the shade of the colonnade and explained that Mr Esquival had already left for his office. Apparently Mrs Esquival didn't eat breakfast, and Abby, who had steeled herself to face a family breakfast similar to the dinner she'd faced the night before, didn't know whether to be glad or sorry.

There was no sign of Alejandro either, which was a relief. When she asked about her brother and his wife she was told that he and *Mees* Lauren usually had breakfast in their rooms. Abby thought that Edward at least might have made an exception in these circumstances. But he was obviously in no hurry to explain himself.

Instead, she had to make the best of it, accepting a serving of scrambled eggs and bacon when the maid offered them against her better judgment. Despite her fears—or perhaps because of them—she was starving, and she consoled herself with the thought that it was after midday back home.

But, with the meal over, the rest of the morning stretched emptily ahead of her. On edge, as she was, she had no interest in the pool. Even the idea of sunbathing on the pool deck reminded her too strongly of what had happened there just a couple of hours earlier. Until Edward decided to show his face she could only wait impatiently for him to appear.

Going up to her room again, she decided to unpack her suitcase, realising that, however much she might want to leave, it wasn't going to happen today. Leaving her clothes in the case would only add to the creases they'd gained on the journey across the Atlantic. And in her present position she didn't want to add to her feelings of inadequacy by looking unkempt.

An hour later she was downstairs again, pacing up and down the terrace, wondering when Edward was going to grace her with his presence, when Dolores Esquival joined her. She paused in the doorway to the salon, looking at Abby a little uncertainly, as if she didn't quite know what she was going to do with her. Abby noticed she was quite clearly dressed to go out.

'Good morning,' Abby greeted her politely, once again cursing her brother for putting her in this position. 'It's a beautiful day.'

'Yes, isn't it?' Dolores hardly glanced up at the cloudless blue sky overhead. Then, linking her hands together at her waist, she added pleasantly, 'Is everything all right?'

As all right as anything could be in the circumstances, thought Abby drily, but she managed a matching response. 'It's fine—everything's fine,' she assured the older woman. Then, because she felt she had to say something more, 'I hope you don't think I was presumptuous in coming here, Mrs Esquival. I really was—worried about my brother.'

Dolores shook her head. 'I am sure you were,' she said, with the first evidence of warmth she'd shown. 'We were worried about him, too. But, happily, he seems to be making a good recovery. We are all hoping his leg heals very soon.'

'Yes.' Abby was grateful for her understanding. 'I—er—I was just waiting for him.'

'Oh, but he is not here,' exclaimed her hostess in surprise. 'I thought you knew. Lauren and Edward's apartment in Coconut Grove was broken into last night. They've gone to accompany the police on an inspection of the property.'

'Oh, no!' Abby immediately felt ashamed of herself for blaming her brother for neglecting her. She frowned. 'Was anything taken? Was anyone hurt?'

'There was no one there, fortunately, and I imagine the police are hoping Lauren and Edward can tell them if anything is missing,' declared Dolores practically. 'Electrical goods are always attractive to thieves, as you probably know, and Edward had—may still have—a very sophisticated entertainment system in the bedroom.'

Abby shook her head. 'Is there anything I can do?'

'I don't think so.' Dolores pulled a wry face. 'If there is any vandalism Luis will arrange to have it dealt with, you can be sure. But of course we will have to decide whether we consider it safe for Lauren to go back there. We will think about that when Edward is on his feet again.'

Abby noticed Dolores was more concerned about Lauren than her brother. But that was only natural. Lauren was an only child, and she was very precious to them.

'I wonder when they'll be back,' she murmured, more to herself than to the other woman. But Lauren's mother had evidently heard her.

'I have no idea,' she said, looking thoughtful. It was as if she'd just realised she couldn't abandon her guest. 'Perhaps you'd better come with me, Abigail,' she decided abruptly. 'I have an appointment at my dress designer's at twelve-thirty but afterwards we could have lunch together. There is a Cuban restaurant close by that serves the most delicious stone crab claws.' She kissed the tips of her fingers in anticipation, her eyes drifting assessingly over Abby's shirt and shorts as she spoke. 'You would have to change, *no,* but…' She shrugged. 'Would you like to see a little of our city?'

Abby wanted to refuse. She desperately needed to talk to Edward, and it had never been part of her plan to make herself anyone else's responsibility. But Dolores evidently expected her to jump at the chance of some sightseeing and, short of pleading tiredness, she couldn't think of a single reason why not.

'I—you don't have to worry about me,' she protested, making a final attempt to avoid the outing, but Dolores was adamant.

'It will be my pleasure,' she insisted, even if she did cast another doubtful look at Abby's appearance. 'Shall we say—twenty minutes? Will that be enough?'

Not nearly, thought Abby a few moments later, riffling through the clothes she'd hung out earlier. Whatever she wore, she was going to look tall and ungainly beside the petite—if plump—Dolores. Why hadn't she pretended to have a head-ache? Surely no one could have argued with that?

But she hadn't, and she had only fifteen minutes left to make herself presentable. On her own, she would have stuck with the shorts. But it was obvious Dolores didn't think they were suitable for a trip to town.

Which left—what? A dress with spaghetti straps that Dolores would probably consider equally unsuitable? Or pants and a vest teamed with a cream suede jacket she'd brought along because it was her favourite?

The pants and jacket won out, and, deciding the plait she'd made of her hair would have to go, she brushed the tangles out, leaving it loose about her shoulders.

She gave one final glance at her reflection before leaving her bedroom. The purple vest was taut across her full breasts, and the beige cotton pants hugged her behind, but she couldn't help that. Thankfully the suede jacket hid a multitude of sins, she thought, even if she was going to feel incredibly hot when she was out in the open air.

The look Dolores gave her when she rejoined the older woman in the reception hall was hardly encouraging, but she ignored it and forced a smile.

'Ready,' she said, realising that Dolores's sky-blue tussore suit had probably cost more than her whole wardrobe put to-gether. 'You look—wonderful.'

'Why, thank you, *cara.*' Dolores evidently appreciated the compliment, though she didn't return it. 'Shall we go?'

They drove to an exclusive little shopping mall in Dolores's car. Dolores herself took the wheel, and Abby was alarmed at the number of near misses they had on the comparatively short journey. Lauren's mother's fingers were never far from the horn, and although some of the almost-accidents were not her fault, Dolores switched lanes indiscriminately, showing little respect for other drivers.

Abby was relieved when they reached their destination. She got out of the car in the busy lot adjoining the mall feeling as if she was lucky to be alive. Even the exhaust fumes that lingered in the sultry air were preferable to the heated atmosphere Dolores had generated and, deciding she was too hot to worry about appearances, Abby slipped off her jacket.

She noticed Dolores gave her bare arms a doubtful look as they crossed the lot to the glass doors that led into the mall. But Abby ignored it. She didn't want to offend her, but she simply wasn't used to the heat.

The doors into the mall were attended by a uniformed security guard, who welcomed them with an obsequious smile. If he wondered who the tall redheaded woman was, he contained his curiosity, greeting Dolores with, *'Señora Esquival Que tal?'* How are you? Almost falling over himself in his eagerness to open the doors.

'Bien, gracias, Tomas,' Dolores responded, sailing past him with barely an acknowledgement of his assistance. She seemed more intent on ridding herself of Abby's presence, saying in a careless tone, 'I am sure you can entertain yourself while I go to the salon, can't you, Abigail?'

Abby expelled a breath. 'Of course,' she said, as relieved as the other woman to have a little time to herself. 'I can meet you back at the car, if you'd rather. You don't have to take me to lunch. I'd be quite happy to go back to the house.'

And see Edward, she added, though only to herself.

Dolores considered for a moment, but, although she might have been attracted by Abby's suggestion, courtesy won out. 'Nonsense,' she said firmly. 'I'm looking forward to it.' Which patently wasn't true. 'The restaurant is at the end of the mall.' She pointed. 'It's called La Terraza. Why don't we meet there in—say, thirty minutes, okay?'

'All right.'

Abby could hardly refuse if Dolores was prepared to put herself out on her behalf. But after the little woman had walked quickly away, swaying a little precariously on her high heels, she wondered how she was going to fill in the next half-hour here. The mall seemed full of designer shops, selling everything from *haute couture* to sports equipment. But everything had a label and the corresponding price tag was out of her reach.

Deciding she could always window-shop, Abby sauntered along the arcade, stopping every now and then to admire a piece of jewellery or a particularly attractive display of evening wear. If you need to ask the price, you can't afford it, she reminded herself drily. Her lips twitched. Evidently her fellow shoppers were far more wealthy than they appeared.

A bookshop offered a welcome escape from the material world. Books, at least, were affordable, and it was interesting to see what novels had made it to the top ten. There were lots of authors she didn't recognise, and she spent quite some time examining the shelves containing crime novels and thrillers. She was wondering if she could buy a couple of books to take home for Ross to read when she glanced at her watch and saw that she was already running out of time.

Dammit! Putting down the books she'd been considering, she hurried out of the store. She had still to find the restaurant, she thought crossly. What had Dolores told her? That it was at the end of the mall?

To her relief, she found the place without difficulty. Fate must have been smiling on her for once, she thought, pausing outside, not sure where Dolores would expect them to meet. She was only seven minutes late, and there was no sign of the other woman. With a bit of luck she might not have arrived yet.

The restaurant itself looked exclusive. But then, she'd expected that. She already knew that Dolores put a lot of stock in appearances. Perhaps she should put her jacket on again, if only to please her.

She was wishing she'd also taken the time to visit the restroom when she became aware that someone was watching her. A man who had been passing the smoked glass doors of the restaurant had paused and was looking at her. And when she turned her head, prepared to give him a cool put-down, she discovered that for the second time that day Alejandro had caught her unawares.

Immediately her pulse went into overdrive, and the dampness she had been feeling at the back of her neck now spread to her hairline. Every pore in her body felt as if it was oozing moisture, and she rubbed a furtive finger over her top lip as he strolled towards her.

'Abigail.' His greeting was polite enough, but she guessed he was remembering their earlier encounter and enjoying her discomfort. 'We meet again.'

Not through choice, I can assure you. Abby bit back the ready retort that sprang to her lips and gave him a thin smile. 'So it seems,' she said tightly, wondering where Dolores was. The other woman had said they should meet *outside* the restaurant, hadn't she? Surely she hadn't sent Alejandro in her place.

Alejandro's dark brows drew together. 'Forgive me,' he said softly, 'but are you waiting for somebody? Edward, perhaps?'

Abby looked up at him and then wished she hadn't. His dark gaze was far too disturbing and she was instantly aware of her own vulnerability where he was concerned. She might hate him, she might despise him for the way he'd treated her, but she could never ignore him. And he knew that, damn him. She could see the awareness glinting in his eyes.

'I—not Edward, no,' she said shortly, wishing he would just go away and leave her. She'd rather attract a stranger's unwelcome attentions, she told herself rashly, than his mocking stare.

'Who then?' he persisted, obviously amused by her red face. '*Que te pasa,* Abigail? What's going on? Surely you are not afraid to tell me?'

'Afraid?' She looked at him again, angry that he should even think such a thing. 'No, of course I'm not afraid, Mr Varga. I just wish you would leave me alone. I'm not Lauren. Nor am I flattered by your attentions. Or the attentions of any man who thinks his wealth gives him the right to have anything he wants!'

Alejandro's face darkened. '*Por Dios*, Abigail, that is unforgivable.'

'Is it?'

Abby was unhappily aware that she had probably gone too far. Edward expected her to be polite to this man, to persuade him to leave Lauren alone, if that was at all credible. Instead of which she was going out of her way to make an enemy of him.

Alejandro took a deep breath now. 'It seems you are determined to believe the worst of me,' he said, flicking back the cuff of his sleeve and glancing at his watch. 'It is almost one-fifteen.' He looked up. 'I suggest you allow me to seat you at my table until your—companion—shows up.'

Abby pressed her lips together, thinking it was a surprisingly conservative watch for someone like him. Slim and gold, perhaps, but it wasn't flashy. Unlike the one Ross wore on his wrist.

'Why should you want to do that?' she asked, unhappy at the turn of her thoughts. Aware, too, of a trickle of moisture sliding down between her breasts. Her nipples felt tight and sensitive and she was sure he must have noticed. Her bra was damp and she might as well have left it at home.

'It is not wise for a woman like you to stand alone in a public shopping mall,' he said now, his dark eyes enigmatic. 'If you were my sister I would not be happy that you are alone. Call it courtesy, if you will. I am merely trying to help you. I would expect your brother to do the same for me.'

Abby made a helpless gesture. 'I'm not waiting for Edward,' she protested.

'No. So you said.' Alejandro's eyes lingered almost palpably on her mouth before moving away. '*No obstante*, my invitation still stands.'

Abby hesitated. Then she said quickly, 'I'm waiting for Mrs Esquival—Dolores. She should be here any minute.'

Alejandro's lean mouth took on a sardonic slant. 'What is

it they say? You should not hold your breath, *no*?' He glanced towards the entrance of the restaurant as the doors opened and a dark-clad man hovered on the threshold. 'Ah, here is Miguel de Brazos. He is the *maître d'* of La Terraza. Allow me to introduce you to your host.'

Abby blew out a breath. 'I don't think—' she began awkwardly, but Alejandro's fingers had slipped about her upper arm, just above her elbow. They were cool against her warm flesh, and unbearably sensual, and she couldn't pull away. In her condition any contact between them would have been sensual, she acknowledged, feeling a little dizzy when Alejandro drew her towards the other man.

He and de Brazos evidently knew one another well, and their rapid exchange in their own language was too swift for Abby to comprehend. Her grasp of Spanish was very limited and Alejandro knew that. She was very relieved when the man stepped forward to greet her in English.

'*Señora,*' he said, with a polite bow. 'You are most welcome. Come.' He gestured eloquently. 'You are waiting for Señora Esquival, are you not? I will have a member of my staff look out for her. It is much more pleasant to wait inside.'

Abby's eyes turned to Alejandro's, but this time he was not looking at her and she was obliged to speak for herself. 'I—that's very kind of you—' she started, grateful for his understanding. But she felt an unwilling pang when Alejandro's hand dropped away from her arm.

'The pleasure is all mine,' de Brazos insisted, taking her answer to mean that she accepted his invitation. Without further ado, he led the way into the restaurant.

Abby glanced back once, but there was still no sign of Dolores. Only Alejandro was behind her, and his expression was inscrutable once more. What was he thinking? she wondered, as the smoky glass doors enclosed them in the cool environs of a palm-shaded lobby. That de Brazos had succeeded where he had failed? Or had this been his intention all along?

The *maître d'* led them to a table at the far side of the

elegantly appointed restaurant. They were seated overlooking a pretty inner courtyard where a fountain played into an ornamental basin. Flowers grew in profusion about the rim, their colours muted by the tinted glass of the windows. But the courtyard was open to the air and birds came to drink from the pool.

It was obviously a favoured spot, and Abby was aware of several pairs of eyes turning in their direction when Alejandro joined her. And, although she told herself that he was completely without shame, she couldn't help but be grateful that he hadn't abandoned her. It would have been rather daunting to wait alone.

'*Que le apetece, señora?* What can I offer you?' de Brazos asked, obviously intending to serve them himself, and Abby drew her upper lip between her teeth as she considered.

'Um—just iced tea for me, please,' she said at last, not trusting herself to drink anything alcoholic in Alejandro's presence. The *maître d'* tutted and pulled a long face.

'Are you sure I cannot tempt you with a margarita, *señora*?' he protested. 'They are the house speciality. I can recommend them.'

Abby shook her head. 'I don't think so, thank you.'

The man arched his eyebrows and turned to her companion. 'And you, *señor*,' he said. 'Will you indulge me?'

'*No lo creo, Miguel,*' Alejandro responded. 'I have work to do this afternoon. I will have iced tea also, *por favor.*'

Miguel spread his hands expressively, but he didn't attempt to try and change Alejandro's mind. He merely inclined his head politely and bustled away, issuing orders to other members of his staff as he went.

There was silence for a few moments after he'd gone, but then, feeling obliged to say something, Abby murmured quietly, 'This is a beautiful restaurant. And this must be the best table in the house.'

Alejandro shrugged. 'I am glad you like it.'

'Who wouldn't?' Abby was feeling a little light-headed now, but she assured herself it was only jet lag, or tiredness, or a combination of both. She studied her jacket uncertainly. 'Do you think I should put this on?'

'*Por que?* Why?' Alejandro regarded her intently. 'Are you cold?'

'No.' Abby glanced expressively around the room, observing the expensively clad patrons with an uneasy eye. Then, speaking almost absently, she added, 'I'm surprised Dolores wanted to bring me here.'

Alejandro's eyebrows ascended. 'And that would be because…?'

'Oh, come on.' Abby forgot who she was speaking to for a moment. 'Haven't you noticed all the diamond bracelets, the strings of pearls, the ruby rings? I'm wearing one ring, one gold chain, and some hoop earrings. I bet your friend Miguel knows their value down to the last cent!'

Alejandro shook his head. 'Perhaps he realises that you do not need diamond bracelets and pearl chokers to accent your beauty,' he responded softly. 'And I do not need to be reminded that you are wearing another man's ring. What do you want me to say, Abigail? That you are still the most attractive woman I have ever known?'

'No!' Abby's face flamed. 'You know I didn't mean anything like that.' Then, aware that her voice had risen and people were looking at them again, she whispered hotly, 'Don't say things like that to me. We both know how insincere your compliments are.'

'Are they?' Alejandro rested his elbows on the table and leaned towards her. 'Would it not please Edward to believe I am still attracted to you? You are very good to look at, *cara*. When Miguel speaks of indulgence, I think of only one thing.'

Abby caught her breath. 'You don't know what Edward wants,' she told him fiercely, choosing the least provocative comment he had made. She cupped her hot face between her palms, wondering why she'd agreed to come here. Where was Dolores? She'd never thought she'd be so eager to see her brother's mother-in-law—but she was.

'I know he did not send for his so-protective older sister to sit beside his sickbed,' responded Alejandro drily, and Abby gave a helpless little moan.

'Then you know more than me,' she retorted, casting another glance towards the entrance. What was Dolores doing? How long did it take to try on a dress?

'You do not make a very convincing liar, *cara*,' murmured Alejandro, relieving her a little by leaning back in his seat. He unbuttoned the jacket of his charcoal suit and hooked a negligent arm over the back of his chair. 'But we will not waste time arguing over your brother.' Absurdly long lashes shaded his eyes as he baited her. 'Tell me about yourself, Abigail. Or tell me why you are lunching with Dolores. I did not realise you were such close friends.'

'We're not.' The words were out before she could stop them, and she hurried to explain what she'd meant. 'That is— Dolores took pity on me. She thought I'd prefer lunching with her rather than just—waiting around at the house for Edward. She'll be here soon. She'll probably tell you the same herself.'

Alejandro frowned. 'Waiting around for Edward?' he said, immediately latching on to the anomaly. 'And why was your brother neglecting you today?'

Abby sighed. 'He wasn't there,' she admitted reluctantly, not really wanting to confide in him. 'He—er—he and Lauren had apparently gone out.'

'Gone out?' Alejandro echoed her words again, and then made an apologetic gesture. 'Forgive me, I thought he could not walk?'

Abby blew out a breath. 'He can't. Not far, anyway.'

Alejandro didn't say anything and, realising she couldn't avoid the inevitable, she said shortly. 'Their apartment has been broken into, if you must know. They've gone to meet the police to assess the damage.'

Alejandro looked less indolent now. 'And when did this— break-in occur?' he asked sharply, and Abby gave him an indignant look.

'Last night, I suppose.' She pretended to be busy folding

her jacket over her lap. 'Why?' She paused, and then added provocatively, 'Do you know anything about it?'

She'd expected an angry denial, but his answer startled her. 'Perhaps,' he said, smoothing his hand over the pearl-grey silk tie which perfectly matched his shirt. 'Perhaps.'

Abby was glad of the distraction of watching that brown long-fingered hand as it moved caressingly against the pale fabric. She was sure if she looked into his eyes he'd see the accusation in hers. Nevertheless, she had to say something, and she was relieved to see the waiter heading towards them. 'I think these are our drinks,' she said, knowing she'd be glad of the refreshment. Her mouth felt suddenly as dry as snuff.

The waiter delivered the two glasses of iced tea with a flourish and then turned to Alejandro to ask if he would like to see the menu.

'*Mas tarde. Later.*' Alejandro inclined his head. '*Gracias.*'

'*Gracias, señor.*'

The waiter bowed and left them and Abby immediately lifted her glass. The ice-cold liquid was both crisp and invigorating, and she closed her eyes for a moment, responding to its delightful flavour. She felt better already, she thought opening her eyes again. Only to revise her opinion when she found Alejandro was watching her.

'You were thirsty,' he remarked, and she almost jumped out of her skin when he leaned forward and wiped a drop of moisture from the corner of her mouth with his thumb. She was even more disturbed when he brought his thumb to his lips and licked the moisture from it, adding swiftly, 'Have you ever drunk wine from a lover's lips?'

'It—it's not wine,' she stammered, too shaken to realise what she was saying, and his thin lips parted in a sensual smile.

'A pleasure I will save for later,' he told her huskily. 'Perhaps you will allow me to buy you dinner tomorrow evening We can continue this discussion then.'

Abby swallowed convulsively. 'I—don't think so.'

'Why not?'

'I—I don't want to,' she said. 'Besides, I don't think my fiancé would approve.'

'As I recall, it did not bother you before,' declared Alejandro obscurely, but before she could take him up on that, or on what he'd meant about the break-in, she heard the sound of hurried footsteps crossing the floor. Abby turned her head. It was Dolores. Of course, she thought defeatedly. Who else would it be?

She stifled a sigh as Alejandro rose to greet his cousin.

'*Querida,*' Dolores exclaimed, capturing his hands and reaching up to bestow air kisses beside his cheeks. 'What are you doing here?' She cast a faintly accusing glance in Abby's direction. 'When Miguel told me you were keeping my guest company, I couldn't believe it. I thought you told me you were always too busy to stop for lunch.'

'Surely you would not have had me leave Abigail standing outside the restaurant, Dolores?' he chided her suavely. 'She looked—lost,' he added, his dark eyes meeting Abby's frustrated gaze with undisguised intent. 'What could I do but offer her myself as a very poor substitute? We have both been waiting anxiously for you to arrive.'

'Oh, Alejandro!' However irritated Dolores might have been at finding them together, his words had successfully diluted any resentment she felt. 'You are so generous! I hope Abigail appreciates your kindness.'

'Oh, I am sure she does,' replied Alejandro, once again looking at Abby with mocking eyes. Then, turning back to his cousin, he added, 'But tell me, *cara*, what is this I hear about your daughter's apartment being broken into? I was most concerned when Abigail told me. Have you heard anything more?'

Dolores immediately lapsed into a torrent of Spanish from which Abby could only distinguish the names of Luis Esquival and her brother and his wife. Whatever Dolores was saying, she evidently didn't want the English girl to interrupt them. It was this as much as anything that caused Abby to remark with contrived innocence, 'Actually, Mr Varga said he might know something about it himself.'

At once Dolores broke off what she was saying to stare at the younger woman. '*Que?*' she said blankly, and Abby was absurdly pleased to see the brief look of irritation that crossed Alejandro's face.

'Mr Varga said he might know something about the robbery,' Abby repeated, widening her eyes. 'That is what you said, isn't it, Mr Varga? I'm sure we're both dying to know what you meant.'

'I believe I said that there might be something I could do to help, *cara*,' he replied smoothly, turning back to Dolores with a reassuring smile. 'Abigail must have misunderstood my desire to be of some assistance.' He cast the culprit a challenging look. 'She knows how fond I am of Lauren—and Edward, too.'

CHAPTER SIX

EDWARD was waiting for Abby when she got back to the house. He was sitting on the terrace, in the shade of the colonnade, his injured leg propped on a cushioned stool. He looked up at his sister belligerently when she came out of the house to tell him she was back.

'Where the hell have you been?' he demanded at once, before Abby could say anything, and her lips parted disbelievingly at the accusation in his voice.

'I've been out to lunch,' she said at last, keeping her tone even with an effort. 'Your mother-in-law took pity on me. It was either that or spend the morning here, on my own.'

'And that would have been a tragedy, would it?' Edward demanded, the freckles on his face standing out against his fair skin. Unlike Abby, he didn't tan, and he looked very pale in these surroundings. 'You didn't come here to go swanning off with Dolores, Abby. As you reminded me last night, this isn't supposed to be a holiday.'

Abby stared at him indignantly. 'Do you honestly think I was eager to go out with Dolores?' she exclaimed. She glanced swiftly behind her, half afraid she might have been overheard, and lowered her voice. 'You didn't tell me where you were going, Eddie. In fact, I got the feeling you were keeping out of my way.'

Was it only her imagination or did Edward look a little shame-faced now? 'Why would I do that?' he asked, making play of adjusting the cushion that was supporting his leg. 'What has Dolores been saying? She's never liked me, you know. As far as the Esquivals are concerned, I've never been good enough for their daughter.'

Abby shook her head. 'Dolores hardly mentioned you,' she

said shortly, irritated that he would try to gain her sympathy
again. 'And after what you asked me to do last night I wasn't
surprised that you'd want to avoid me. But don't think you're
deceiving Alejandro. He knows what you're trying to do.'

Now there was no doubt about Edward's agitation. 'He
knows?' he echoed faintly. 'How do you know that?' He
pushed himself up in his seat, almost overbalancing the stool
in the process. 'Have you seen him?'

'Yes—'

Abby had been about to explain that he'd come to the house
earlier that morning, but Edward didn't allow her to go on.

'Where did you see him? Was Dolores there when he mentioned me?' A sheen of sweat stood out on his forehead. 'Oh,
God, if the Esquivals find out what's going on, I'm dead!'

Abby was confused, and it showed. Surely if Lauren was
having an affair it was she who should deserve her parents'
censure, not Edward.

Unless…

Studying her brother's anxious face, Abby had the sudden
premonition that he wasn't being honest with her. But what
was it that he wasn't telling her? What did Alejandro know
that he thought might cause the Esquivals to turn against him?

Deciding this was not the time to get into that, she pulled
out a nearby chair and sat down beside him. 'Anyway,' she
said, trying to be upbeat, 'tell me about your morning. Dolores
said your apartment was broken into. Was there much damage? What did they take?'

Edward made an offhanded gesture. 'What do they usually
take?' he asked dismissively. 'Break-ins happen. You know
that. It was probably some druggie, looking for something he
could sell for a fix.'

'Is that what the police think?'

'How should I know what they think?' Edward didn't seem
interested. 'No one tells me anything.'

Abby refused to answer that. Taking another tack, she said,
'Ross's house was broken into last year. They never did find
who did it. Like you say—'

'Like I'm interested in your boyfriend's problems,' muttered Edward rudely. 'Let's get back to Varga. Are you going to explain how you came to be talking to him? Did he invite himself for lunch with you and my so-delightful mother-in-law?'

Abby shook her head. She had thought she'd deflected any discussion of Alejandro, but she should have known better. And why was Edward so worried about what the other man might have said?

She knew Alejandro wasn't to be trusted. Look how he'd deflected her accusation at lunchtime. Dolores had virtually apologised to him for what he'd implied was Abby's mistake. Only it hadn't been a mistake. She would swear it. Alejandro had intimated that he might know something about the robbery at Edward's apartment. But what? *What?*

'He—met us outside the restaurant,' she replied at last, deciding not to mention his earlier visit. 'He joined us for a drink, that's all.' She paused. 'What is this all about, Eddie? If Lauren is having an affair with Alejandro, why are you so upset about what her parents might think? It's not your fault.'

Edward's head jerked towards her. 'Is she having an affair with Varga?' he exclaimed, clutching her hand with sweating fingers.

'I don't know.' Abby pulled her hand away with a feeling of distaste. 'It was you who said she was.' She sighed. 'Perhaps you'd better start being honest with me, Eddie. Why are you so afraid of Alejandro? It's not just because of Lauren, is it?'

'What else could it be?' Edward had stiffened at her words and now he glared at her with angry eyes. 'And I'm not afraid of Varga.' He paused. 'Only of what he might—do.'

'To your marriage?'

'What else?' Edward was defiant. 'Anyway, why did you say he knows what I'm doing? What did he say to give you that impression?'

Abby shrugged. 'I don't remember,' she said, deciding if Edward could be evasive, so could she. But that didn't stop her from wishing she'd never started this conversation. Edward was lying to her. She was almost sure of it now. Perhaps she ought to speak to Alejandro himself.

Edward was looking infuriated now, but Abby was not inclined to humour him. 'We'll talk later,' she said, getting to her feet. 'I need to change. I'll see you in a little while.'

'Wait!'

Edward tried to catch her hand, but she was too quick for him. Wrapping her arms about her waist, she hurried into the house, running up the stairs to her room with a feeling of total isolation.

Abby rang Ross before going down for dinner.

She'd spent the remainder of the afternoon in her room, going over both what Alejandro had said and her brother's reaction to it. But she was no further forward. Alejandro's attitude had been enigmatic; Edward's had been downright defensive. Or should that be apprehensive? There was no doubt that he'd been alarmed when she'd told him Alejandro had joined her and Dolores for a drink.

She shook her head. She hardly remembered what Alejandro had said now. Only that there had been a definite air of menace in his words. Why would he presume that Edward needed his assistance? The two men obviously despised one another. What could there possibly be between them to have caused such an unlikely alliance?

Herself? No! Edward knew nothing of what had happened after she'd returned to England. Lauren? She was unwilling to accept that either. Yet why? Didn't she want to believe Alejandro was capable of having an affair with her sister-in-law? Was she jealous, perhaps? Even after all this time did she still harbour feelings for him herself?

No!

Staring at her reflection in the mirror above the vanity unit, Abby dismissed the suggestion out of hand. Edward might dislike Alejandro; she *hated* him. She'd hoped she'd never have to lay eyes on him again.

Nevertheless, it was thinking about Alejandro that persuaded her to ring her fiancé again. She needed Ross's advice,
she thought eagerly. She needed his cool voice of reason to
still the chaotic turmoil in her head.

To her relief, he answered the phone at the first ring. Which
meant he was probably sitting at his desk in his study, she
reflected, marking papers that he'd brought home from school.

What she'd give to be back there with him, she thought.
She might even revise her decision not to move in with him
until after they were married. Continuing to live in her own
apartment when she spent so much time at Ross's house
seemed foolish from this distance. She had to learn to trust
him. He was going to be her husband, for goodness' sake.

'It's me, Ross,' she said brightly, after he had identified
himself. 'I hope you don't mind me ringing so late.'

'It's only eleven o'clock, Abby,' he retorted, his tone hardly
boding well in the circumstances. 'I was expecting you to ring,
actually. I knew you'd want to apologise for the way you
spoke to me this morning.'

Abby blew out a breath. Until that moment she'd forgotten
the argument they'd had earlier. She'd been so wrapped up in
Edward's problems she'd ignored the fact that she'd probably
offended her fiancé.

But she should have known he wouldn't forget, and it was
easier to give in than risk more hostility. 'Yes,' she said ruefully, somehow managing to keep the resignation out of her
voice. 'I shouldn't have said what I did. I'm sorry. But I have
been worried about Eddie, you know.'

'Mmm.' Ross didn't sound as if he thought that was any
excuse. 'So, what's going on? Have you made any arrangements yet for coming home? Or is that asking too much?'

'It is, rather.' Abby wished he could be more understanding.
She needed his support, not his censure. 'There have been—
more complications.'

Ross snorted. 'Let me guess: Edward's had an emotional
relapse?'

'No.' Abby kept her temper in check with an effort. 'His

apartment—the apartment he shares with Lauren—was broken into. Last night, I think. It's just not what he needs when he' practically incapable of doing anything for himself.'

'I don't believe it.' Ross was impatient. 'That man is walking disaster, Abby. Or in this case an *un*walking one.'

'That isn't funny, Ross. Couldn't you try and show a littl sympathy? Remember how you felt when your house was van dalised last year.'

'That was different.'

'How was it different?'

'Oh, Abby…' Ross sighed. 'I have some valuable thing here—things that are precious to me, that were my mother': I doubt if your brother owns anything he couldn't replace the nearest supermarket.'

Abby gasped. 'That's a horrible thing to say,' she ex claimed, although she was uneasily aware that he might b right. Edward had seemed decidedly blasé about the robbery He'd dismissed it in a few words, she remembered, more con cerned about Alejandro than anything else.

'I'm only trying to be practical,' said Ross, and Abby ha to admit that that was why she'd called. She'd wanted Ross' practicality. It was a pity it seemed so cold when it was pu into words.

'Even so…'

But Abby sounded defensive, and, as if sensing her weak ness, Ross changed his tack. 'I'm only thinking of you, swee heart,' he said, his voice softening. 'I'm sure the authoriti have the situation under control. And you have to rememb Edward has a wife and in-laws to support him. I need yo here, Abby. I miss you. I really do.'

'I miss you, too,' said Abby automatically, yet in truth she' had too much else on her mind. 'But I can't leave yet, Ros I can't. Not until I'm sure Eddie can cope.'

'Can cope with what?'

Ross's voice had risen and Abby knew there was no wa she could justify her reasons for staying on to him. He didn know Alejandro. He didn't know anything about what ha happened the last time she'd visited her brother. All he knew was that she'd been ill after she'd got back from Edward's wedding. So ill that she'd been away from school for several weeks after her return from Florida.

She sighed now. 'Just give me a few more days, Ross,' she pleaded. 'I've hardly spoken to Lauren yet. Things have been so hectic today that we haven't found time to talk.'

'To talk!' Ross sounded incredulous. 'You're not trying to tell me you want to stay on because you and your sister-in-law haven't had the time to exchange all the latest gossip?'

'No, of course not.'

'It sounds that way.'

'Well, I'm sorry for how it sounds,' said Abby tiredly. 'In any case, I'm staying on until after the weekend at least. I'll ring you tomorrow if I have any more news.'

Ross was silent, and she thought at first he wasn't going to say anything else. But then he expelled a weary breath. 'I hope you know what you're doing, Abby,' he said heavily. 'Letting Edward think he can call on you every time things don't go his way doesn't seem very sensible to me.'

And it wasn't, thought Abby unhappily, after she'd ended the call. She'd always been a push-over where her brother was concerned and he knew it. But this time she was really worried about him. Even the injuries he'd received in the car accident seemed incidental compared to all the rest.

She'd undressed and was about to get in the shower when the phone rang again.

Ross, she guessed wearily. She'd had to give him this number and he was probably ringing to reinforce his contention that she ought to return home. Couldn't he just cut her some slack, here? She groaned, clutching a towel about her. She was tired and anxious and his constant carping wasn't helping at all.

'Okay, it's me,' she said, after picking up the receiver, and then nearly dropped the thing when an unexpected voice spoke in her ear.

'Am I supposed to be flattered that you anticipated my call?'

Alejandro enquired softly, and Abby despised the sudden quiver of excitement that feathered down her spine at his words.

She swallowed. 'Ale—Mr Varga!'

'As I do not believe you were about to say alleluia, Alejandro will do,' he told her drily. 'That is obviously how you think of me. And why not? We know one another rather too well to stand on ceremony.'

Abby sucked in some air. 'What do you want, Alejandro?' she demanded shortly and she heard his small sigh of regret.

'So cold, *cara*,' he murmured. 'Is this what your Englishmen have done to you? You used to have such a lust for life.'

'Whereas you—' Abby broke off before she said something unforgivable. Then, determinedly, 'Why did you ring, Alejandro? Aren't you afraid that the Esquivals might be curious about why you're contacting me?'

'Why should I care what my cousins think?' he replied carelessly. 'I do not have to ask their permission to speak to an old friend.'

'We were never friends, Alejandro,' Abby blurted, too tired to be tactful, and then shivered uncontrollably when he gave a soft laugh.

'I am glad you agree,' he said. 'We were not friends, we were lovers. Like me, I think, you cannot forget what we shared.'

'We didn't share anything,' Abby broke in desperately. 'I don't know why you're doing this, Alejandro, but I wish you'd just leave me alone.'

'Do you?' Alejandro hesitated. 'Is that what your brother wishes also?'

Abby gasped. 'Leave Edward out of this.'

'Unfortunately, I cannot.' Alejandro gave a regretful sigh. 'Is that not why he sent for you? Because he hopes you may succeed where he has failed?'

Abby stiffened. 'Failed?' she echoed. What was he admitting? 'Failed at what?'

'Ah...' Alejandro sounded as if her confusion had pleased him. 'You do not know. I thought that must be true.'

'Know what?'

'That is for me to know and you to find out,' declared Alejandro tormentingly. 'So—you will have dinner with me tomorrow evening. We will continue this discussion then, *no*?'

'No!'

'Oh, I think you will, *cara*,' he told her softly, and again she felt that little twinge of menace she'd felt that morning by the pool. 'Do not make me angry, Abigail. Your brother would not like it. After all, he wants us to be—friends.'

Abby's hands trembled and she badly wanted to slam down the phone. She was no match for a man like Alejandro. She didn't know what he was or what he was capable of. He was Edward's problem, not hers. She was getting too far out of her depth.

'Please,' she said, and she despised the beseeching note she could hear in her voice, 'tell me what this is all about.'

'Tomorrow evening,' said Alejandro inexorably, and she didn't know whether it was a threat or a promise. 'I will tell Luis and Dolores that we were discussing sailing at lunch today and that I have offered to show you my boat, *sí*? They may be—surprised, but that is not your concern.'

Abby blew out a breath. 'I'm their guest,' she protested. 'I can't just have dinner with you. What will they think?'

'At least you are no longer refusing to consider my proposition,' remarked Alejandro sardonically. 'Leave the details to me, *cara*. I will see you tomorrow. *Adios*.'

CHAPTER SEVEN

DINNER that evening was a more relaxed affair.

The robbery at the Coconut Grove apartment was the main topic of conversation, and although Edward had been dismissive of it earlier he now appeared to be as willing to talk about it as everyone else.

Or perhaps that was just because Lauren and his in-laws expected that of him, reflected Abby broodingly, aware that she was getting very cynical about her brother's motives for anything. It didn't help to see him sitting there, looking as if he was innocent of any wrongdoing, when he must know that the Esquivals believed Abby had invited herself here.

'At least they didn't trash the place,' said Lauren fervently. She turned to her sister-in-law. 'Perhaps you'd like to come and see it tomorrow. The music centre and the TV are missing, of course, but the rest of the apartment is okay.'

'Which proves they were only after items they could easily sell,' observed her father, before Abby could respond. 'Like Edward said earlier, they were most probably kids looking for ways to make money to buy drugs.'

'I don't think they were kids,' Lauren insisted, glancing at her husband almost defensively. 'Kids couldn't have got in without setting off the alarm.'

'So what do you think it was?' Edward asked scornfully. 'A professional hit?'

'It could be.'

Lauren wasn't deterred, and Abby sensed that she had doubts about the break-in. Edward, meanwhile, was avoiding his sister's eyes, and she wished she didn't have the feeling that he had his own reasons for not pursuing that line of thought.

'*No obstante*, I am not at all happy about Lauren returning to the apartment,' declared her mother staunchly. 'Do you not agree, Luis? If these—thieves—can get in once, they may get in again.'

'*Es verdad.* That's true,' agreed her husband sagely. 'What do you think, Abigail? Have you heard that villains often return to the scene of the crime? Particularly if they think the insurance company has paid for the stolen items to be replaced, *no*?'

Abby wasn't at all happy about being put on the spot, particularly as she suspected her brother had his own reasons for wanting to return home. But Luis was waiting for her answer and she shrugged. 'I've heard that, too,' she admitted, giving Lauren a sympathetic look. 'But perhaps if you fitted a new alarm—'

'That's a good idea, Papá,' said Lauren at once. 'And if it was teenagers, as Edward thinks, they probably won't bother us again.'

'That's what I think,' said Edward, and Abby wondered why he seemed so keen to play the incident down. Did he have something to hide? Surely he hadn't arranged to have the apartment burglarised himself.

But, no. As Abby determinedly put such thoughts aside, Luis's aunt chose to make her own contribution. 'Why do we not all wait and see what *la policia* come up with?' she remarked mildly. 'I am sure Abigail does not wish to spend her holiday discussing our little problems.' She paused. 'How are you enjoying your stay, *pequeña*? Dolores tells me you and she had lunch together at La Terraza. Did you know that I used to work at La Terraza? When I was a much younger woman, *naturalmente*.' She smiled.

'What Tia Elena means is that her husband's family used to own La Terraza,' Dolores explained shortly, clearly eager that Abby shouldn't get the wrong impression. She gave the old woman a reproving look. 'It is a great pity that they decided to sell. These days it is making a fortune, *no*?'

'Money is not everything, Dolores,' returned the old lady, undaunted. 'I think you forget that sometimes.'

'I forget nothing, Tia,' retorted Dolores quellingly. She lifted the bell beside her plate and rang it imperiously, speaking in rapid Spanish to the maid when she arrived. Then, after the girl had cleared their plates, she said, 'Shall we go into the salon? I have asked Anita to serve coffee in there.'

Abby got the chance to talk to Lauren after they'd all adjourned to the salon. The younger girl had settled herself on a hide-covered sofa set at right angles to the huge fireplace and Abby hesitated only a second before taking the seat beside her.

She noticed that Edward didn't look particularly pleased that she'd chosen to join his wife, but that couldn't be helped. He shouldn't have told her Lauren was having an affair with Alejandro Varga if he'd wanted to keep it a secret. Besides, Abby had no intention of asking her about that. She just wanted the opportunity to gauge for herself exactly what was going on in her brother's marriage.

Lauren herself looked slightly surprised when Abby sat down, but she was too polite to offer any objection. On the contrary, she immediately struck up a conversation, asking Abby about her engagement, admiring her ring and proffering the suggestion that she and Ross ought to consider returning to Florida for their honeymoon.

Abby, knowing full well that Ross would never agree to such a thing, made some neutral rejoinder before saying lightly, 'It seems no time since we were discussing your honeymoon, Lauren. But I suppose you and Edward are quite used to being married now.'

'Y—e—s.' Lauren drew out the word in such a way that Abby was hardly reassured. 'We are happy enough, I suppose. Though this has not been an easy year for us.'

'No.' Abby nodded understandingly. 'I suppose the accident was quite a shock.'

'It was.' Lauren accepted a cup of coffee from the maid before continuing. 'But that isn't what I meant.'

'It's not?' Abby was aware that her brother was watching them with a lowering expression. She moistened her lips. 'I'm sorry. I didn't mean to pry.'

'It's not your fault.' Lauren hesitated. 'Oh, I suppose I should not say anything to you. But you are Edward's sister. You have a right to know.'

Abby wondered if she did. And if this was about Alejandro she didn't think she wanted to know. Though how else was she to learn the truth? She had the feeling Lauren wouldn't lie.

'Has he said anything to you?' the younger woman persisted, and Abby had no idea how to answer her.

'I—Edward and I haven't had a lot of time to talk about anything,' she murmured evasively. 'What with the break-in and all.'

'Por supuesto.' Of course. Lauren circled the rim of her cup with a nervous finger. 'And I suppose it is not an easy thing for him to tell you.'

This was getting worse and worse. Abby, glancing at her brother, was uneasily aware that she might have misjudged him all along. It sounded very much as if Lauren was trying to break it to her gently. Had Lauren been having an affair? And, if so, with whom?

'You—er—you don't have to tell me if you don't want to,' Abby said quickly. 'Honestly, I—'

'But I want to tell you,' said Lauren firmly. 'Perhaps you will understand my feelings better than your brother. Now that you are going to be married yourself.'

Abby wanted to say *Don't hold your breath*, but her mouth was too dry to allow more than a strangled gulp to escape her.

Lauren seemed to take her silence as acquiescence, however. Setting her cup on the low table in front of them, she said quietly, 'You see, Edward and I have been having some—personal—problems.'

Oh, no! Abby was convinced now that she didn't want to hear this. 'Really…' she began again, recovering her voice. 'I don't think I am the person you need to talk to.'

Lauren gave her a thoughtful little look. 'Perhaps that is so,' she conceded softly. 'I forget—things are different in your country, are they not?'

Abby didn't quite know what she meant by that, but she thought it was wiser not to probe. Obviously Lauren couldn't talk about this to her mother and father. Still, why she should think her sister-in-law might view her behaviour more sympathetically, Abby didn't know.

Or want to, she assured herself. It was bad enough having Edward unloading all his troubles onto her shoulders. She couldn't take on Lauren's as well.

'Did I tell you Alejandro joined your mother and Abby for a drink at lunchtime?' Edward asked suddenly. He had propelled himself across the room to where they were sitting and now perched on the arm of the sofa at his wife's side. 'He's very fond of Abby. They met at our wedding, you know.'

His wife looked up at him with narrowed eyes. 'No, you did not tell me,' she said, a wary note entering her voice. She turned back to Abby. 'I did not realise you knew Alejandro so well.'

'I don't,' said Abby shortly, wondering what her brother was playing at now. 'Edward's exaggerating.'

'I don't think so,' he said annoyingly. 'He was certainly delighted to renew your acquaintance yesterday, as I recall.'

Abby's eyes bored into his. 'Mr Varga was simply being polite, that's all,' she said tersely. And then, remembering that she was supposed to be having dinner with Alejandro the following evening, she cursed Edward anew for getting her into this situation. She clenched her fists. 'You know him better than I do.'

Edward was undaunted. 'Do I?' he challenged. 'I wouldn't say that. I shouldn't be at all surprised if he wants to see you again before you leave.'

Abby's face burned with embarrassment. Was he only guessing that Alejandro had been in touch with her? She could tell little from his expression, and she didn't know whether to be glad or sorry when Dolores chose that moment to stroll across the room to join them.

'Who wants to see you, *cara*?' she asked, touching her daughter's shoulder with a gentle hand, and Lauren looked up at her mother with some misgivings.

'Not me, Mamá,' she said tautly. 'Abigail. Edward has just been telling me that Alejandro had a drink with you both at lunchtime.'

'Well, yes. He did. But I do not understand.' Dolores frowned. 'What are you saying?'

Abby stifled a groan. In spite of the fact that her brother had presented her with the perfect opportunity to tell them all about Alejandro's invitation, she couldn't speak. Not after what Lauren had just told her. Not after she had virtually admitted that she was involved with another man.

'I was just saying that it was possible that—Alejandro—' and, although Abby was dismayed at his audacity, she sensed the effort it took for Edward to use his name '—that he might like to see Abby again before she leaves,' he continued, his words dropping into the sudden silence like pebbles into a still pool. 'What do you think, sweetheart?' He laid a possessive hand on his wife's arm, as if challenging her mother's protection. 'Didn't you get the feeling that he was unusually pleased to see her the other day?'

'But Abigail hardly knows Alejandro,' protested Dolores, before her daughter could speak.

'They spent some time together when Abby came over for the wedding,' Edward countered, despite the look his sister cast his way. 'And now that he's divorced the situation is different. There's no reason why they shouldn't be friends.'

Dolores was not pleased. 'Alejandro is a busy man,' she said tightly. 'Abigail should not be deceived by his very obvious charm.' She turned to Abby. 'I'm sorry if this sounds unfeeling, Abigail. But Alejandro can't help flirting with the ladies.' She forced a smile to soften her words. 'He's very naughty sometimes, but I'm afraid he treats us all the same.'

'Not all of us, Mamá,' Lauren contradicted, glancing up at

her husband, and Abby wondered if that was a tacit admission of her own guilt or something else. 'And we don't know what Alejandro thinks of Abigail. We are not in his confidence.' She turned her dark eyes on her sister-in-law now. 'Perhaps we should ask her.'

Abby hadn't expected this. 'I'm not in his confidence either,' she averred quickly. 'Like your mother says, I hardly know him.' *And what I do know, I don't like,* she finished silently, wishing Edward would stop embarrassing her. 'Um— would you mind if I said goodnight now? It's been a long day and I'm afraid my body's still working on London time.'

Abby spent the following morning with Lauren and her mother, visiting the Coconut Grove apartment.

The two women seemed to think last night's discussion about Alejandro required no further explanation, and Abby couldn't help a certain frisson of resentment that they had dismissed any connection between her and Alejandro out of hand.

Not that she wanted them to think that she was attracted to him, she assured herself firmly. She had quite enough to deal with as it was.

She would have found Coconut Grove itself delightful if she'd been more in the mood to appreciate it. The district was one of Miami's oldest, with lots of fabulous shops and boutiques and restaurants crammed into a comparatively small area. She guessed it would really come alive after nightfall, when the old-fashioned streetlamps were lit and the music swelling out of its bars and cafés took on a darker rhythm. But even in daylight it possessed a warmth and character that was different from even its closest neighbours.

Edward and Lauren's apartment was part of a restored complex surrounding a central open-air mall. Although the old buildings had been extensively modernised inside, outside they maintained their essentially Spanish appearance. Stucco-washed walls and tiles in different colours; palm trees growing in pots in the courtyard; narrow wooden balconies with white-painted rails.

If you could overlook the evidence that the place had been dusted for fingerprints, the apartment itself was cool and attractive. A large living area opened onto one of the balconies Abby had seen from below, and Lauren was quick to point out that they could see the tropical gardens and the marina from their windows. Adjoining the living room was a small kitchen, with every conceivable domestic appliance, but Abby guessed from its appearance that her brother and his wife seldom cooked at home.

Lauren proved to be surprisingly enthusiastic about returning to the apartment. 'It is our home,' she said, showing Abby into the master bedroom with its impressive king-sized divan. She pointed out the damage that had been done when the entertainment centre had been ripped from the fitted armoire at the foot of the bed. 'This can easily be repaired,' she added, paling a little at the sight of such blatant savagery. Then, determinedly, 'And I know Edward does not like living at my parents' estate.'

Abby agreed with her, although she could quite see why Lauren's mother felt so apprehensive about their return. And Dolores, bustling into the room at that moment, clicked her tongue at the shattered cabinet and splintered wood lying about the floor.

'You cannot think of coming back here, Lauren,' she exclaimed fiercely. 'Imagine what might have happened if you had been here alone when these men broke in. You could have been murdered in your bed!'

'They might not have attempted the break-in if we had been here,' declared her daughter practically. 'It probably only happened because the apartment was unoccupied. You never know, someone at the restaurant may have mentioned that Edward had had an accident and that for the time being we were staying with you and Papá.'

Dolores widened her eyes impatiently and then looked at Abby, almost as if she blamed her for her daughter's words.

'Well, I think your *Papá* should find you another apartment,' she stated tersely. 'Somewhere in Coral Gables, nearer to where we live.'

'I am not a child, *Mamá*.' Lauren drifted back into the living room, running a possessive hand over the back of a printed silk sofa. 'Besides, apart from a few dirty footmarks, the rest of the apartment is hardly touched. It's obvious they were in a hurry and only took what they could easily sell.'

Abby had been inclined to agree with her—until she saw the expensive laptop lying on a shelf beside the long windows. A thief surely would not have left the portable computer behind. Unless it had been overlooked. She supposed that was possible. But it was curious, and she intended to ask Edward what the police had said about it.

'I do not think we should talk about this right now,' said Dolores shortly, following them back into the living room. 'It's much too soon to be making any plans. Edward is unlikely to be able to walk unaided for several weeks yet.' She turned to Abby, evidently expecting her support. 'A man needs to be fit enough to defend himself and his family. Especially after what has happened. Do you not agree?'

Abby looked at her sister-in-law and then made a helpless gesture. 'I suppose,' she said awkwardly. 'But it's up to Edward and Lauren to decide when they want to return home. I understand your concerns. But if the police are satisfied…'

'The *policia* know no more than we do,' retorted Lauren's mother impatiently. 'It may be that someone is conducting a vendetta against Edward. How do we know?'

Abby felt a chill run down her spine at these words. And almost without her volition the memory of Alejandro's taunting arrogance caused a prickling to feather her skin. Was he behind this? Did he have some hold over her brother? Oh, God, she was going to have to have dinner with him, whatever her feelings. She had find out once and for all what was going on.

CHAPTER EIGHT

To ABBY's dismay, Alejandro was waiting for them when they got back to the villa.

He and Luis were sitting on the terrace, enjoying a cold beer, and both men rose politely to their feet when the three women appeared.

Lauren and her mother greeted Alejandro with great enthusiasm, a circumstance Abby was getting used to. And if they, like she, noticed that Edward was absent, they were too busy welcoming their guest to comment.

'Are you staying for lunch?' asked Lauren eagerly, clearly reluctant to let go of his hands, and, meeting Alejandro's gaze over the younger woman's shoulder, Abby saw the familiar mockery glinting in his eyes. Why was he here? she wondered. Was it just because he and Luis had business to discuss? Or had he some other motive? Making sure she didn't turn down his invitation, perhaps?

'Regrettably, no,' he replied now, using the ruse of ushering her into the chair he had been occupying to release himself. Reaching for his beer, he emptied the bottle in one swift swallow and set it back on the table. 'As a matter of fact I came to ask Abigail if she would care to come and see my boat this evening. It cannot have been much fun for her to learn that her brother had been injured. And now, with the break-in and all, I thought she might appreciate a diversion.'

Abby's lips compressed, and she was aware that both Dolores and her daughter had turned to give her a considering look. What were they thinking? she wondered. That they would all appreciate a diversion? And why had she ever thought that Alejandro might leave the decision of whether she accepted his invitation or not to her? He was a determined man. She knew that already. And an unscrupulous one, she added tensely. But the most frustrating thing of all was that she didn't dare refuse.

'Well, I—' she began, groping for words. Lauren interrupted her. 'I think we'd all enjoy an evening on the water,' she said, voicing the thought Abby had had. 'I assume we are invited, too. I don't know about my husband, but I'd certainly like to go.'

'You forget, *cara*, we are already committed to staying in this evening,' remarked Edward suddenly.

Abby swung round to find her brother propped against one of the vine-covered pillars that supported the colonnade. He was evidently enjoying their surprise, and he smiled at his wife disarmingly. Then, hooking the crutches beneath his arms, he moved jerkily towards them.

With a sideways glance at Abby, he went on smoothly, 'I believe your mother told me that your aunt and uncle are joining us for dinner, Lauren. I know Tia Rosa would be terribly upset if her favourite niece was absent.'

Lauren's mouth pursed. 'I had forgotten that,' she said, looking disappointed. She turned to her mother. 'Couldn't we possibly postpone Tia Rosa and Tio Ernesto's visit? After all, Abigail will be leaving soon. It seems a shame to deprive her of this opportunity to see Alejandro's yacht.'

'I'm sure Alejandro can be trusted to look after my sister without a chaperon,' said Edward at once, and Abby wished she had the nerve to tell him to butt out of her affairs. The trouble was, she knew she had to go. She had to find out what Alejandro wanted. She had to know what was really going on.

'Perhaps Abigail would prefer to spend the evening with the family,' put in Dolores, making her sympathies known, but Luis chose to come down on Edward's side.

'We were not invited, *cara*,' he said, the smile he gave Alejandro salving any offence. 'I am sure my friend would prefer it if Abigail was allowed to make her own decision.'

Abby wished she didn't have to make any choice at all, but that was not an option. 'I—it sounds delightful,' she said, hoping both Alejandro and Edward could hear the irony in her voice.

'It will be; I can assure you,' murmured the Cuban suavely. 'Shall we say—seven o'clock this evening? I will send a car to pick you up.'

Abby spent ages trying to decide what to wear. She wished now that she'd taken advantage of her trip to the mall with Dolores to buy something suitable for herself. But then she hadn't known Alejandro was going to take her sailing. Was she a good sailor? Her experiences with boats had been confined to pleasure steamers and cross-channel ferries.

She would have preferred to wear one of the two dresses she'd brought with her. But they were hardly appropriate for climbing on and off a yacht. The last thing she wanted was for him to think she'd chosen glamour over practicality, even if deep down inside her she wanted to look good.

Telling herself it didn't matter what he thought of her, she chose her one remaining pair of shorts. She'd bought them the previous summer in Rimini, and although when she'd got them she'd doubted she'd ever get the chance to wear them, they seemed appropriate tonight.

They had been extremely expensive, she remembered, and Ross had balked a little at her extravagance. Made of a rich emerald-green silk, with a gold-plated chain belt to hang loosely about her hips, they were obviously far too formal for casual wear. But probably ideal for what she wanted tonight.

Teamed with a black crêpe halter-top, she couldn't deny they suited her. She looked pretty good, she thought, turning sideways in front of the long mirrors, trying to see herself from behind. Too good, in fact, for going out with a man she purported to despise, she conceded. Her mouth compressed into a thin line. What was she thinking of?

She was crazy, she thought. Worse than that, she was betraying everything she had ever believed about herself. Not to mention her fiancé. Dear Lord, she could imagine how he'd react if he could see her now.

With an exclamation of distaste, she took hold of the two
sides of the halter, ready to pull it over her head again when
someone knocked at her door. She faltered. What now? It was
barely a quarter to seven. She still had to apply her lipstick
and put the finishing touches to her hair.

'Who is it?' she called, standing irresolutely in front of the
mirror. Then closed her eyes in frustration when the maid
opened the door.

'Carlos is waiting, *señora*,' she said, her eyes widening in
both surprise and admiration. '*Por favor*, will you come?'

Abby expelled a resigned sigh. 'Just give me a couple of
minutes,' she replied, realising there was no time to change
her clothes now. 'I won't be long.'

'*Sí, señora.*'

With another lingering stare, the maid departed, and Abby
turned back to the vanity, stifling a curse. Well, she was committed now. For her sins, she had to accept her fate.

Predictably, Edward was in the hall when she went downstairs. Probably ensuring that she didn't duck out of the date,
she thought irritably. She just wished she could have been
wearing jeans and a tee shirt, or something equally casual.
Instead of which she could practically feel the satisfaction oozing out of his pores.

'Hey, way to go, Abbs!' he exclaimed approvingly.
'Varga's not going to know what's hit him.'

'Oh, grow up, Eddie,' retorted Abby, in no mood to humour
him. 'I just hope there's not more to this than you've told me.'

Edward scowled. 'I don't know what you mean,' he said
defensively. 'All I came to say was that I hoped you'd have
a pleasant evening. I'm sure you will. If there's one thing
Varga's good at, it's giving a woman a good time.'

'And you'd know all about that, would you?' Abby arched
her brows sardonically. 'Just don't say anything else, Eddie. I
may just decide to develop a migraine instead.'

Of course, she knew she wouldn't. She couldn't. And he
knew that, too. But that didn't stop her from enjoying his

uncertainty and the automatic look of anxiety that crossed his face.

She was glad none of the Esquivals appeared as she crossed the hall to the open doors. She'd had to wear her sandals again, in the absence of any alternative, and her high heels clattered on the marble floor. But, happily, no one seemed to notice. She was able to descend the steps without attracting attention.

Outside, the air was like a moist blanket. Heat, soft and palpable, coated her bare arms, and the scents of a dozen flowering shrubs filled the night with promise. If only she'd been going out with Ross, or even Edward, she thought ruefully. She would have enjoyed this so much more.

Or would she?

The traitorous thought was quickly squashed as she greeted Carlos, who was standing holding the door of the limousine. 'Evenin', ma'am,' he responded politely, his expression impassive. Then, after closing the rear door behind her and sliding in behind the wheel, 'You okay?'

'As I'll ever be,' murmured Abby to herself, before saying brightly, 'Yes, thanks. Are you?'

'Hey, I'm always okay,' said Carlos good-humouredly. He met her eyes in the rearview mirror and grinned. 'You sure look good tonight, Ms Leighton.'

Abby couldn't help feeling pleased. Even if he was confirming her fears that Alejandro would think she'd gone to all this trouble for him. Which she supposed she had, she admitted unwillingly. But there were limits to what even a designer outfit could do.

'Um—I hope my outfit is suitable for sailing,' she ventured, aware that it probably wasn't wise to question the chauffeur. 'I understand Mr Varga owns—a boat.'

'That he does, ma'am,' Carlos agreed. 'His daddy was into shipping in quite a big way. Mr Varga—he's into all sorts of things. But I expect you know that for yourself.'

Abby sighed, not prepared to admit how little she did know. 'So where are we going?' she asked, glancing out of the windows. At night everything looked different, and she had no idea where they were now.

'Well, not to the shipyard, ma'am,' he drawled wryly. 'Mr Varga, he wants me to bring you to his house. 'Course, he does have a cruiser in his backyard,' he added thoughtfully. 'I'd say that's what he has in mind.'

Abby hardly heard a word beyond the fact that they were on their way to Alejandro's house. She sank back in the seat and blew out an indignant breath. How dared he? she asked herself furiously. He must know what going to his house would mean to her. But then, when had he ever considered her feelings? She should have known better than to put herself into his hands.

But then something else Carlos had said impinged on her consciousness. 'What did you mean about him having a cruiser in his backyard?'

Carlos's eyes moved briefly to the mirror. 'I guess you've never been to Mr Varga's house,' he drawled easily. 'It's on the water. He keeps the cruiser at his dock.'

Abby blinked. 'But I thought—' She stopped herself and began again, 'Isn't his house on Old Okra Road?'

'No way. Mr Varga's daddy used to have a house on Old Okra, but he moved into a retirement community a couple years ago. I guess that's how you got the wrong address.'

'I guess it is.'

Abby frowned, not sure whether she was glad or sorry. Either way, Alejandro hadn't mentioned dining at his house.

She realised now that they were driving south of the city. Away to her left she could see the lights of Key Biscayne, and she seemed to remember Edward telling her that this road ran all the way to the Keys. Surely that wasn't where they were heading? There were over a hundred miles of causeway between the mainland and Key West, which was geographically closer to Havana than Miami. But then, Alejandro's origins did lie with the Cuban community, too. Perhaps he felt more at home with his father's people.

But before she could begin to panic Carlos turned off the

main highway into the quieter streets of the suburbs. They crossed Old Cutler Road, bypassed the tropical gardens, and headed towards the coast. Carlos opened his window a crack and she smelled the tang of the ocean. The breeze that invaded the car was refreshingly cool.

Alejandro's house was at the end of a narrow lane, where palms and rioting hibiscus hung over every wall. Unlike at the Esquivals' estate, the iron gates that led into the property stood wide, and in the lights of the car's headlights Abby saw that only a pair of stone griffins guarded the entrance.

Carlos turned skilfully between the gates and brought the big car to a halt before a rambling two-storeyed residence that was almost completely covered with flowering vines. It was evidently a much older property than the house on Old Okra Road, with a slightly Twenties appearance. It reminded Abby of Norma Desmond's house in *Sunset Boulevard*, and she wouldn't have been at all surprised to see a vintage Studebaker parked in the shade of the ancient oaks that cast their shadows over the already sombre driveway.

It wasn't at all what she'd expected. The other house had had a much grander appearance, with a soaring roofline and glass everywhere. This house was totally different, and although carriage lamps provided some illumination, its appeal lay in the air of mystery that surrounded it like a cloak.

Carlos barely had time to get out of the car and swing open her door before the porch door opened and a shaft of golden light speared out from within. Alejandro stood in its brilliance, his expression hidden by the halo of light behind him. But in a wide-sleeved white shirt and tight-fitting black pants, his open collar just hinting at the darkness of the flesh beneath, his identity was unmistakeable.

Abby quivered. She couldn't help it. This was so much the way she remembered him. She had to fight back the urge she had to step out of the car and walk into his arms.

But that was crazy; *she* was crazy. Whatever Alejandro wanted, it wasn't her body. He had invited her here to talk about Edward and perhaps about Lauren. He was obviously as fond of his cousin as she was of him. So why was she sitting here wishing things—wishing life—could have been different? *Get over it, Abby,* she told herself. *Alejandro Varga was never meant for you.*

With a feeling of sudden helplessness she moved across the seat and thrust her foot out onto the crushed shell drive. Her sandal sank into the surprisingly soft surface, and she guessed the humidity seldom dried out here. Then Alejandro stepped forward and took her hand, and she was powerless to stop him from raising it to his lips.

His mouth was moist, too, his breath—or was it his tongue?—dampening her skin, and she shivered again. She should never have agreed to this, she thought unsteadily. Never have come here. Talk about walking into the lion's den.

'*Bienvenido,*' he greeted her softly. 'Welcome to my home. It is good to see you again, *cara*. I have been waiting for this moment for so long. Please.' He gestured behind him. 'Come in.'

'You didn't say we'd be having dinner at your house,' whispered Abby accusingly, but Alejandro only lifted enquiring eyes to the chauffeur, who was still waiting by the car.

'You can go, Carlos,' he said without inflection. 'I will call you if your services are required later. *Adios, amigo.* Have a good evening.'

'*Gracias, señor.*'

Abby was aware that the man looked at her before leaving. What was he thinking? she wondered. Did he have any sympathy for her plight? Had he any idea how much she longed to be leaving with him? That even returning to the Esquivals would be better than this?

Safer, certainly. But it was too late to be having second thoughts. Alejandro's fingers had fastened about her upper arm and he was guiding her across the forecourt and up the steps to the porch. Leading her, irresistibly, into his house.

A polished brass chandelier cast its light over the amber and black tiles of the entry, and beyond silk rugs in jewelled shades complemented dark wood panelling and rich satin drapes. The house was cool, but not excessively so, and Abby's skin cooled rapidly. The mingled scents of a dozen tropical blooms gave the air a heady fragrance.

A staircase wound to the upper floor of the house, but Abby averted her eyes quickly. Before she started to wonder whether Alejandro's bedroom was anything like the one in his father's house. In any case, he was guiding her into a spacious living room, and she forced herself to pay attention to that instead.

Three velvet sofas surrounded a flower-filled hearth that was richly patterned. Carved oak cabinets contained a veritable fortune in *objets d'art*. Trumpet-shaped orchids and delicate magnolias spilled from porcelain bowls and crystal vases that matched the chandelier sparkling above her head.

There were high-back chairs set against the walls, and lots of paintings, and an ornate bureau that was obviously an antique. Once again, the colours were vivid, but subtle, and Abby was reminded of her earlier notion. It was evident that the house was even older than she had thought.

But it wasn't sensible to allow herself to be overwhelmed by her surroundings, however beautiful they undoubtedly were. Alejandro hadn't brought her here to admire his house or his possessions. He'd brought her here for his own reasons, and she'd be wise to remember that.

To distract herself, she pulled away from Alejandro and moved to the long windows at the far side of the room. The sliding doors that led out to the deck were closed, but tall iron lamps set amongst the surrounding foliage illuminated the scene. The lights winked between the moving fronds of palm trees and added radiance to the bougainvillaea that tumbled from the balcony above.

There was a lizard, too, on the wooden railing. It seemed mesmerised by the light that came from the house. It waited, motionless, hoping to blend in with the vegetation, its little pulse beating rapidly in its throat.

Alejandro's shadowy reflection showed that he'd come to stand behind her, and she was as instantly aware of him as of the faint draught of cool air from the vent above her head. At once the encroaching greenery beyond the windows seemed to trap her, between its rampant vegetation and the subtle menace of the man at her back.

CHAPTER NINE

BECAUSE she needed to say something, anything, to break the spell he seemed to cast so effortlessly over her, Abby hurried into speech. 'Carlos said this house is on the water,' she said, keeping her eyes on the lizard, with whom she felt a certain affinity. 'Is—is the ocean visible from here?'

She could hear the mild amusement in his voice as he answered her. 'No,' he said indulgently. 'This whole coastline is honeycombed with small bays and waterways. My dock is on Turtle Creek. Biscayne Bay is about half a mile away.'

'Oh.'

Abby was trying desperately to think of something else to say when he murmured, 'And to answer your accusation earlier: I do not recall telling you where we were going to have dinner.'

'No, but—' She'd turned before realising how unwise that was, and she was forced to take a backward step to keep a sensible space between them. Even so, she was intensely conscious of his nearness, and of how dark his skin looked against the whiteness of his shirt. 'That is—you must have known what I would think when—when Carlos told me where we were going.'

'No.' Alejandro was deliberately obtuse. 'Why do you not tell me?'

Abby shook her head. 'Don't play games, Alejandro. You knew I'd think we were going to the house on Old Okra Road.'

'But the house on Old Okra Road is not my house.'

'I know that now.' Abby was infuriated by his ability to behave as if he was incapable of any deceit when she knew only too well he was. 'But you didn't tell me it wasn't your house. Carlos did.'

Alejandro pushed his hands into the back pockets of his trousers. 'Good old Carlos,' he said drily. 'Tell me, *cara*, is this going somewhere?'

Abby pressed her lips together for a moment, controlling her impatience. 'As I said before, you like playing games, Alejandro. But I don't.'

'Which means...?'

'It means you deliberately let me think the house on Old Okra Road was your house,' she retorted tensely. 'But of course you couldn't take me to your house, could you? Your wife wouldn't have liked it. And that was something else you forgot to tell me.'

Alejandro's nostrils flared, and for a moment his dark features looked almost sinister. 'I suppose Edward told you,' he said harshly. 'Your dear brother, who is as culpable for keeping secrets as I am, it seems.'

Abby met his challenging gaze only briefly. It was hard to sustain her composure in the face of such blatant hostility, and she was uneasily aware of how vulnerable she was here. This was Alejandro's house, Alejandro's territory. He could say—and do—what he liked.

'Edward did tell me you were married,' she admitted at last. 'Do you blame him? I am his sister, after all. He was only looking out for me.'

'That must be a first,' remarked Alejandro, swaying back on his heels before turning and walking away from her. And before she could think of a suitable retort he stopped beside a cabinet and swung open the doors to reveal a comprehensive wet bar. 'What will you have to drink? And please do not say iced tea because I do not have any. Wine, perhaps, or a cocktail? You choose.'

Abby caught her upper lip between her teeth. Then, realising she wasn't going to get anywhere if she behaved sullenly, she shrugged. 'Do you have a spritzer?'

Alejandro gave her a resigned look. 'No.'

'Wine, then,' she said tightly. 'White wine, if you have it. Just a small glass.'

'I was not about to give you a tumbler,' he responded drily. 'And, yes, we have white wine. Is a Californian Chardonnay all right?'

As Abby was seldom able to tell one white wine from another, she could hardly object. But because he had been so sarcastic she said, 'I suppose so,' and had the satisfaction of seeing the way his mouth tightened at her words.

The appearance of a white-clad steward provided a welcome diversion. The man spoke to his employer in Spanish, and because he was obliged to deal with the enquiry Abby was able to take her glass from Alejandro's outstretched hand without worrying too much about whether their fingers touched or not.

In fact, they didn't, but that didn't prevent her from feeling grateful for the interruption. The atmosphere had been getting increasingly intense and it was good to breathe normally again.

Deciding she might feel safer if she was sitting down, Abby took the initiative and seated herself in a tapestry-covered armchair. She chose the chair deliberately rather than one of the sofas. Sitting on a sofa was an invitation for him to join her, and despite her efforts to keep their association on an impersonal level Alejandro seemed determined to thwart her.

'Your drink is all right?'

She realised abruptly that while she'd been lost in thought the servant had gone away again and Alejandro was now standing right in front of her. Unfortunately, as well as intimidating her, it put her eyes on a level with the impressive bulge of his manhood. Averting her eyes again, she took an unwary gulp of the wine in her glass and almost choked as it went down the wrong way.

Red-faced and embarrassed, she was obliged to take the napkin Alejandro offered her, and was frustratedly aware that he'd probably stood over her deliberately, knowing exactly how on edge she'd feel.

But just as she was considering how best to deal with the

threat he posed he seemed to take pity on her. Crossing the room, he sat down on one of the dark red velvet sofas she'd admired earlier. Hooking one deck-shoed foot across his knee—she noticed inconsequently that he wasn't wearing any socks—he draped one arm along the back of the sofa before raising the glass he was carrying to his lips. It was a tumbler, and she wondered if the colourless liquid in the glass was water or something stronger. Either way, it was obvious that he was perfectly at ease with himself, and it infuriated her anew that she should be such an easy mark. All the same, she was grateful for the respite that the distance gave.

'Feeling better?' he asked now, his deep voice with its distinctive Cuban accent scraping across her raw nerves. She was instantly aware that she was achieving nothing by putting off the inevitable. She had to talk to this man; she had to find out what he wanted. But most of all she had to stop making it so easy for him to control the conversation.

'Yes, thank you,' she answered, taking another sip of her wine just to prove that she could. Then, setting her glass down on the coaster he'd placed on a nearby table, she forced herself to look at him. 'Have you lived here long?'

His mouth compressed, as if he knew exactly what she was thinking, but he was coolly indulgent when he replied. 'The house used to belong to my aunt. When she died, it came to me.'

Abby hesitated. 'Was that before or after you got your divorce?' she asked crisply, and had the satisfaction of seeing his eyes darken with an irritation he couldn't hide.

'After,' he said eventually. 'My ex-wife never lived here, if that's what you want to know.' Then, with equal audacity, 'When did you break your engagement? Was that before or after you got back from the wedding?'

Abby blinked. 'I—' She was nonplussed. 'Who told you I'd broken my engagement?'

'Guess,' he said drily, and her brows drew together in total confusion.

'But—I only got engaged two months ago,' she protested. 'Why would I—?'

But she didn't complete the sentence. Suddenly something else he'd said came back to her, and she stared at him uncomprehendingly. 'What wedding are you talking about?'

Alejandro's lips twisted. 'How many weddings have you and I attended?'

'Edward's wedding!' she said incredulously. And, at his curt nod, 'I wasn't engaged when Eddie got married.'

'So it was before,' said Alejandro harshly. 'I should have known your brother wouldn't tell the truth.'

Abby gazed at him. 'I don't know what you're talking about,' she declared coldly. Then, holding up her head, she added, 'In any case, I didn't come here to talk about me. I came to talk about Eddie. I'd like to know why you persist in accusing him of—of God knows what when—when you're the—the—'

'Villain?' he supplied mockingly, but she ignored him.

'—the transgressor here?' she finished primly. 'I'm glad you're not denying it.'

Alejandro's expression softened. 'You really do not know, do you, *cara*?' he mused. 'What has he told you, I wonder? What explanation has he given you for his—what shall I call it?—his hostility towards me?'

'Don't pretend you don't know,' she exclaimed at once. 'You—you can't keep your hands off his wife. Why wouldn't he be hostile towards you when you're trying to destroy his marriage?'

Alejandro made a strangled sound and she thought for a moment he was choking. But he wasn't. She quickly realised he was fighting the desire to laugh, and it infuriated her that he could find it funny. This wasn't a game. This was her brother's life, his future. But then, what could she expect from a man who'd betrayed his own wife?

Abby wanted to get up and walk out of there. But she didn't. She couldn't. Now that it was out in the open, she owed it to Edward to try and put things right. Whatever hold the Cuban had over him, surely it could not withstand the exposure of Alejandro's treachery? He'd had it all his own way for far too long. It was up to her to level the score.

But to her dismay Alejandro had put down his glass now and got to his feet again. She steeled herself for a confrontation, but instead of coming towards her he went to stand by the windows, looking out onto the floodlit deck as she had done earlier.

'Bien,' he said softly. 'So that is what he has told you. And you believed him. I do not know whether to be flattered or insulted, *cara*. What do you think?'

Abby swallowed, aware that he had turned his head and was looking at her now, but she couldn't back down. 'I think you should be ashamed,' she said tensely. 'I would be, in your shoes. Lauren—Lauren must be young enough to be your daughter.'

'Or my niece,' agreed Alejandro, without expression. He shook his head incredulously. 'I would have to be very desperate or very stupid to regard my good friend's daughter in that way.'

Abby turned her head now. 'Are you denying that you're having an affair with her?'

'Denying it?' Alejandro echoed the words disbelievingly. *'En que piensas!* What are you thinking! The question is not a serious one. I am not interested in Lauren Esquival.'

'It's Lauren Leighton,' put in Abby quickly, and he sighed.

'Lauren Leighten, *sí,*' he amended flatly. *'Por Dios*, Abigail, she is a child. A trying child at times, *a lo mejor*. But a child, *no obstante.'*

Abby got unsteadily to her feet. 'Of course, you would say that.'

'Yes, I would.' He turned right round now, and suddenly the space between them didn't seem half as safe. *'Cristo*, are you listening to me, Abigail? Lauren is charming—amusing, even. But I have never touched her. I treat her as I would a younger sister. I have never been attracted to her.'

Abby swallowed, trying to concentrate her attention on the

brown flesh rising from the unbuttoned neckline of his shirt. 'I—I hear what you say,' she said, noticing the pulse that was beating in his throat. His heart appeared to be racing just as hers was. But in his case it was probably frustration, whereas she was fighting an awareness that was rapidly overwhelming her good sense.

Alejandro stared at her for a long moment and then, just as she'd feared, he strolled back to where she was standing. *'Pobrecita,'* he said huskily. 'You hear my words but you do not believe me. You know in your heart it is the truth, but for your brother's sake you tell yourself you are not convinced.'

'Do you blame me?' She expelled a nervous breath. 'And if you're trying to intimidate me, Alejandro, you're succeeding.'

'Hijo de puta!' he swore softly. 'I am not trying to intimidate you, *cara.* I am trying to make you understand that there is more going on here than you think.'

Abby pressed her lips together. 'I've known Eddie all his life—'

'Which means what, exactly?'

Abby shook her head. 'I—I would know if he was lying to me.'

'Muy bien.' Alejandro shrugged. 'And what if I told you he is afraid to tell the truth? What then?'

Abby swallowed. 'Eddie's not afraid of you,' she exclaimed unsteadily, but her words sounded hollow even to her own ears.

'I did not say he was afraid of me,' said Alejandro softly, lifting his hand almost involuntarily and drawing his knuckles along the stiff line of her jawline. 'Must I say it again, *cara*? I am not Edward's enemy. Whatever he may have told you, it is not true.'

She jerked back from his touch, but, as if her action had achieved the opposite of what she'd intended, he didn't withdraw his hand. Instead, he allowed his fingers to trail over her throat to the low vee of her halter, sliding beneath the cloth, his nails gently scoring her skin.

Abby felt weak. In spite of everything that had happened, she was suddenly overwhelmed by needs she'd assured herself were consigned to oblivion. Memories of the night he'd made love to her came flooding into her consciousness, and his touch was unbearably real, unbearably familiar. His nearness, the warmth of his breath, his hands, were stripping away her defences, and she knew if she didn't move soon she wouldn't be able to move at all.

'I think you'd better let me go,' she said, hearing the underlying panic in her voice and praying that he couldn't detect it. 'This isn't going to work.'

His smile was enigmatic, but she guessed he knew exactly how feeble her boast was. The truth was, it was succeeding all too well, and when she put out her hand to ward him off she found her fingers caught in his tormenting grasp.

'I fear Edward knows how wrong you are,' he breathed, and to her dismay he brought her hand to his lips. His tongue brushed her palm and she felt its sensual caress in every quivering nerve of her body. Hot and dark, his sexuality poured over her, and when he spoke again she had to concentrate hard to understand what he was saying. 'He knows I still want you, does he not?' he murmured thickly. 'That is what he has told you. That I would—how would he say it?—ditch Lauren, *no*, if I thought I could have you?'

'Don't be so ridiculous!'

Abby dragged her hand away from his, scrubbing it violently against her hip. Yet she could still feel his tongue, still feel his heat enveloping her. Oh, God, she thought unsteadily. Why had she ever thought she could do this? Why had she let Edward persuade her that Alejandro would listen to her?

To her relief, however, Alejandro didn't pursue it. She didn't believe he'd accepted defeat. That was unlikely to be his way. He was probably only saving himself for a future confrontation. He knew as well as she did that she wasn't going anywhere right now.

'Come,' he said abruptly, turning back to the windows. He

offered her his hand, but this time Abby knew better than to take it.

'Where are we going?' she asked, trying to keep the tremor out of her voice, and he smiled.

'To the dock, of course,' he said, unlatching the sliding doors and stepping aside to allow her to precede him. 'I want to show you my boat.'

His boat! Abby took a calming breath. She'd forgotten why he'd invited her here. And she so much didn't want to leave the comparative safety of his house.

'I—don't know,' she said, making no move to join him. 'I'm not a very good sailor.'

'You will not have to be,' he told her firmly. And she wondered if he thought that anything he said would reassure her.

'Alejandro—'

'Come,' he said again, with just a trace of impatience in his voice. 'Would you disappoint your brother? He wishes for me to be so infatuated with you that I will do whatever he wants.'

CHAPTER TEN

ALEJANDRO'S boat was both more and less than Abby had anticipated.

It was smaller, certainly: a forty-foot vessel, with two masts gracing its shining teak deck. There were living quarters below that were both conservative and comfortable. But it wasn't the gleaming steel yacht Abby had expected. Like his house, it possessed charm and character instead.

They'd reached the dock by walking through a lush paradise of ferns and palms and creepers. Delicate orchids with trumpet-shaped petals had brushed her cheeks and waxy magnolias and vivid hibiscus grew in wild profusion, their scents alone heady and overpowering. Abby had been almost glad when Alejandro placed a firm hand in the small of her back to guide her over a particularly uneven patch of ground. Her head had been spinning, and it wasn't just the intoxication of the flowers.

She'd been intensely aware of his nearness. Of how easily he had overpowered her. But she had also been aware that the tropical undergrowth might hide other exotic specimens that were less attractive. Snakes and spiders, for example, although she doubted she was in any danger here.

Nevertheless, she'd been relieved when they had stepped onto the ribbed planking of the dock and she'd been able to free herself both from Alejandro's hold and the fears that had pursued her from the house. Yet now, when Alejandro went past her to check on the mooring lines, she found herself watching him again, admiring the tight curve of his buttocks as he bent to pull on the ropes. All his movements were lithe and sensual, she admitted. He seemed to possess a dark power she was unable to resist.

Dear Lord!

She dragged her eyes away from temptation and found herself gazing instead into two eyes staring at her from the darkness of the creek. They seemed to float just above the surface of the water, their appraisal heavy-lidded and intent.

A little squeak of alarm escaped her. She was sure it was an alligator, and she glanced in panic around the dock. Fortunately, it was built well above the water, to accommodate Alejandro's boat, but she could easily imagine the reptile crawling up the bank towards them.

Alejandro straightened at the sound of her cry. He turned quickly towards her and she realised she was probably making a fool of herself again. The creature, whatever it was, had disappeared beneath the surface of the water, and there was no way anyone could identify it in the creek's murky depths.

'Is something wrong?'

Alejandro came towards her, and despite the fact that she'd calmed her fears Abby wished she dared clutch his hand. 'It's nothing,' she said hurriedly, though her eyes still searched the reeds that grew in such profusion along the waterway. 'I—' She had to say it. 'I thought I saw an alligator.' The lamplight revealed his wry expression as she added, with some embarrassment, 'But I'm sure it wasn't. And it's gone now, in any case.'

'So what do you think it was?' he asked, arching his dark brows enquiringly.

'I don't know.' She was sure he was making fun of her again, and she refused to let him see he had her spooked. 'A fox, maybe. Or a raccoon. You have them here, don't you? But it was in the water. I just saw its eyes watching me.'

Alejandro smiled. 'And you think it was admiring its supper before eating it, *bien*?' he mused softly, and she gave him an indignant look.

'I knew you wouldn't take it seriously,' she said, wrapping her arms about herself. 'Well, I'm not used to wild animals in my backyard.'

'Nor am I, *cara*,' he assured her softly. 'And I am sorry if you did not like my joke. But I doubt if it was an alligator, *mi amor*. Alligators do not usually scare my guests.'

'So what was it?'

Alejandro shrugged. 'A manatee, perhaps,' he replied considering. 'There used to be many of them about here. Regrettably the propellers of speedboats have made them an endangered species.'

'Oh.' Abby stared at him. 'That's awful!'

'It is also life,' said Alejandro drily. 'Or should I say death? You have a soft heart, *cara*. I like that.'

No, I'm just soft, thought Abby, not knowing how to answer him, and she was relieved when Alejandro changed the subject.

'Shall we go aboard?' he suggested, indicating the gangway he'd attached to the bow. He glanced at her feet. 'But perhaps you should take off your shoes, *no*? I would hate for you to lose your balance and fall into the creek with our uninvited guest.'

Abby glared at him. She hadn't had any option when it came to her choice of footwear, and she was perfectly well aware of how ridiculous her sandals must appear to him. He probably thought she'd worn them to impress him, she thought resentfully, and she kicked off her heels with some irritation.

'Much better,' he observed softly, and although he wasn't looking at them her toes curled just the same. He had a way of speaking to her that caused the fine hairs on the back of her neck to prickle in anticipation, and she was again reminded of the night they had spent together.

Brushing past him, she made for the gangway. She wanted the evening over, she told herself. And once he realised that he was wasting his time baiting her he'd surely get to the point of this meeting.

He followed her aboard and the boat rocked alarmingly on the swell. But, although she half expected him to take advantage of her momentary unsteadiness to touch her, he just moved ahead into the pilot's cabin and switched on the generator.

Almost immediately lights flowered all over the vessel and Abby caught her breath at the beauty of polished wood and shining brass. A steep stairway led down into the stateroom and Alejandro came out of the cabin to indicate that she should follow him.

She would have preferred to go ahead rather than follow him. It meant she had to expose herself to his enigmatic gaze. But he was already descending the steps with the ease of familiarity, and, dropping her sandals onto the deck, she grasped the handrail and started down.

Keeping her eyes firmly on her feet, and not on his dark upturned face, she looked about her. Below deck was just as impressive as above. A galley was situated to one side and a narrow companionway gave access to the main cabin. Beyond that, she guessed, were the sleeping quarters. But that was definitely something she didn't want to think about now.

There was the delicious scent of cooked food, but a brief glance into the galley convinced her that no one had been cooking there. As with Lauren and Edward's apartment, the kitchen looked untouched, and she was therefore unprepared for the sight that met her eyes when she stepped into the stateroom.

A long buffet table had been laid beneath the square windows, and the scents she had detected earlier evidently came from here. Everything was steaming hot, and she could only assume that while she and Alejandro had been having their drinks at the house a veritable army of servants had been working tirelessly. How long had it taken, she wondered, to set this up?

'I hope you like Cuban food,' murmured Alejandro half apologetically, and she shook her head in total disbelief.

'It—smells delicious,' she said hastily, realising that he might misinterpret that reaction. Then, because she couldn't remain angry with him when he'd obviously gone to so much trouble on her account, she added softly, 'You'll have to tell me what everything is. Apart from stone crabs, I don't think I've tried Cuban food before.'

'O—kay.' The word sounded strange coming from his lips but his smile was genuine enough. 'Let me introduce you, hmm?'

He collected a fork from the display and invited her to join him beside the table. Then, dipping the fork into a concoction of saffron-flavoured rice and peas, he skewered an enormous shrimp and offered it to her.

It was delicious: fleshy and sweet, and dripping with a rich creamy sauce. '*Camarones,*' Alejandro said, indicating the shrimp. He watched her bite into it with obvious enjoyment. 'You like, *sí?*'

'*Sí.*'

Abby dabbed at her chin with a napkin, aware that she probably shouldn't be enjoying herself. But she was. Nevertheless, letting him take her to dinner was one thing. Letting him feed her from his own hand was something else.

The next thing he offered was a golden-brown roll that she'd assumed was made of potato but wasn't. Delicious curls of ham delighted her tastebuds as she bit into it. Mixed with shredded vegetables and fried to a consistency that was crisp on the outside and juicily soft within, it was both sweet and spicy. It reminded her of fritters she'd tasted at home.

'*Croquetas,*' he said, once again enjoying her pleasure. Then, with disturbing intimacy. 'Has anyone ever told you what a delight you are to please, *cara?* So many women would starve themselves before they would eat this food.'

Abby grimaced, wiping her mouth. 'What are you saying? That I'm a lost cause?' she asked. She was gazing longingly at the crisply roasted chicken he had chosen next, and Alejandro's brows drew together in confusion.

'*Que?*' he said. 'I do not know what you mean?'

'That I'm fat?' suggested Abby wryly, and he made an astonished sound.

'You are not fat, *cara,*' he said huskily. 'And I should know, *recuerda?* Remember?'

She remembered, but now was not the time to be thinking of that. Not when he was so near, when he was being so nice.

and when she was definitely in danger of forgetting why she was here.

'Um—what's this?' she asked, moving away from him along the table, and to her relief he accepted her attempt to change the subject.

'That is *ropa vieja*,' he told her lightly. 'A shredded beef stew. And the spicy-smelling dish beside it is gumbo, which is not a Cuban speciality at all. It actually comes from the Cajun district of southern Louisiana, but I like it and I am hoping you will like it also.'

Abby was very much afraid that she liked everything— which wasn't very wise when the dishes she was being offered were all rich in carbohydrates and served in heavy sauces. She dreaded to think how many calories she was consuming. But the food didn't seem to have done Alejandro any harm, she reflected ruefully, and stopped worrying about her diet and just indulged herself.

As well as all the spicy dishes there were other things to tempt her. *Plátano*, which was deep-fried banana; crème caramel Hispanic-style, cooked in a crisply baked pastry shell; Florida's own key lime pie and fruits of every kind.

They eventually filled their plates and retired to the cushioned banquette that circled the bow. From here long windows gave an uninterrupted view of the creek, where the dancing lights of vessels out in the bay glinted in the darkness.

Alejandro put some Latino music on the hi-fi, and the exotic rhythms of salsa and merengue couldn't help but fire her blood. Sometimes the beat was fast, but at others it was slower and sensually appealing. It was music to dance to or make love to, and her senses wavered at the prospect of doing either of those things with Alejandro.

Even so, she was relaxing. Slowly, but surely she could feel the tension in her body slipping away. Alejandro had made no move towards her and she was half inclined to believe that her awareness of him was exaggerated. He was certainly doing his best to put her at her ease.

Nevertheless, she was aware that the wine might have something to do with it. Despite her misgivings, it would have been churlish to refuse. But it was certainly heady stuff, and she'd drunk several glasses. By the time the meal was over she was feeling decidedly muzzy.

But pleasantly so, she assured herself, unable at that moment to find the energy to worry about it. She was enjoying herself too much, and she didn't want to spoil it by thinking about anything else.

Edward!

Her brother's face swam before her eyes and she blinked determinedly. That was why she was here: to talk about Edward. Nothing else. She was letting herself be seduced by the night and the wine and the music—and the man, she thought impatiently. She should never forget the reasons that had brought her here.

Or the man who was to blame.

Alejandro.

She started when he got to his feet, but he only collected their plates and went aft to deposit them in the galley. Then he was back again, holding out his hand towards her, inviting her to get to her feet.

He expected her to dance with him, she realised, disbelievingly. Just as she was preparing herself to confront him, he was following his own agenda again. And this time there was no escape. Setting her wine glass aside, he pulled her up from the banquette. Before she knew what was happening, she was in his arms.

'We have to talk,' she protested, feeling the heat of his fingers through the thin fabric of her top. His thumb brushed the bare skin above the back of the halter and she shivered. 'Alejandro, I don't want to dance with you. That's not why I came.'

'No.' He conceded the point, but he didn't let her go. 'But that does not mean we cannot enjoy ourselves, *cara*. Trust me. We will get to what you want in good time.'

Trust him? Abby felt a hysterical desire to laugh. Yeah, right, she thought wildly. She could do that. She'd done it before and look where it had got her. She wouldn't be here at all if she hadn't made the mistake of trusting Alejandro before. How could he ask her to trust him when she didn't even trust herself?

Nevertheless, when he started to move in time to the music it was incredibly difficult to keep that in mind. The night, the hypnotic rhythm of the music, the lean strength of his body moving against hers, sent her senses reeling. His hand was in the small of her back, pressing her even closer. If she relaxed and leaned into him would she feel the hard length of his manhood against her stomach?

But that was madness. They were dancing, not indulging in some illicit foreplay to sex. Yet sex was in her mind; sex was all she could think of. Dear God, how much wine had he fed her? What had been in it to make her feel almost wild with desire?

She felt dizzy, disorientated. Being here with Alejandro seemed unbelievable, unreal. When she dared a glance up at him she glimpsed a matching anguish in his expression. But then it was gone, replaced by the mocking sensuality of his smile.

Watching her intently, he slid his fingers between hers and brought their hands close to his body. Now she could feel the sinuous movement of his leg as he moved against her, and he deliberately pressed her hand against his thigh.

'Do you want to feel what you do to me, *cara*?' he breathed against her ear before catching the gold hoop of her earring between his teeth and tugging gently on it. 'Or perhaps you are not ready to share that with me yet.'

'Alejandro—'

The word was choked. She wanted to tell him that she'd never be ready to share anything with him, but he only gave a soft laugh and swung her round.

The cabin spun wildly about her. She couldn't keep her balance, and she groped for his shoulder, needing something solid to hold on to. But his shirt was smooth and silky, and instead of grasping a handful of the cloth her fingers slid onto his neck.

She snatched her hand away at once, but not before she'd registered warm, slightly damp skin, and dark hair that curled about her fingers. And recognised the fact that he was as sensitive to her touch as she was to his.

'*Querida,*' he said huskily, pressing her free hand against his groin. Then, skimming both hands up her arms, he took possession of her shoulders. 'Do you have any idea what I am thinking at this moment? Do you know how often I have imagined this moment in my dreams?'

'Alejandro—'

'Even the way you say my name is different from anyone else,' he continued, his thumb massaging the curve of her jawline. 'Do you remember how it was with us? Do you remember that night as well as I do? We could not get enough of one another, *cara*. And you—you tasted so good—'

'Stop it!'

Abby almost choked on the word. This couldn't be happening. Was he completely shameless? Was she? She was an engaged woman, for heaven's sake. Didn't that mean anything to him? Didn't it mean anything to Edward either? she wondered desperately. She rather thought the answer had to be no, on both counts.

'You do not mean that, *cara*.'

He didn't believe her. She almost groaned. Why was she not surprised? Whatever Edward thought, she was not prepared for this. Nor was she prepared to—to prostitute herself because her brother thought it might give him some advantage. What was going on? Why was nobody telling her the truth?

She realised suddenly that Alejandro was nuzzling her neck. She felt his teeth against her skin and her own flesh betrayed her. When he bit her, when he sucked an inch of skin into his mouth and drew on it with hard, purposeful lips and tongue, she couldn't suppress the helpless moan that escaped her. God, it felt so good, and she felt the wet heat of her own arousal between her legs.

'Esto te gusta?' he asked her thickly. 'Do you like?' His hands were gripping her midriff and she realised that he was touching her bare flesh. The halter had separated from her shorts when he'd spun her around, and his fingers dipped into her waistband to probe the sensitive hollow at the base of her spine. *'Tu eres muy hermoso, cara.* You are very beautiful. But you know this. I have told you many times before.'

Yes, he had. And she'd believed him then. To her cost. She didn't believe him now. He was only playing with her. He was seeing how far she would go, how far she would let *him* go. And somehow—somehow, God help her!—she had to call a halt before it was too late.

'Please, Alejandro,' she begged, despising herself for pleading with him. 'You said—you said you would do what I wanted if—if I agreed to dance with you. Well, we're not dancing now.'

'You think not, *cara*?' His tone was softly sensual. 'But surely this is the oldest dance there is.'

'I don't understand you.' But she did. She understood him only too well.

'No?' Alejandro's eyes searched her face. 'You surprise me, *cara*. Well—let me show you how it is with me.'

He bent his head then, and although she turned her face aside his lips grazed the corner of her mouth. It was not a forceful kiss. His tongue barely touched her cheek. But she felt it deep down in the knotted core of her stomach, and, despite everything she'd been telling herself, she couldn't prevent the wave of longing that swept over her.

And he knew it, damn him. Knew that if he kissed her again, if he parted his legs and drew her close enough to feel the unmistakable stirring of his erection, she would not be able to resist him. The fight was an unequal one. She wasn't only fighting him, she was fighting herself.

He did kiss her again, his hand at the back of her head guiding her mouth to his. His tongue swept between her lips, exulting in her submission, and she could no longer pretend that she wasn't participating in her own seduction. She was drowning in sensation, and this time she couldn't blame the wine.

He kissed her over and over, slanting his mouth across hers as if he wanted to drag the very breath from her. Her lungs were labouring and she was dizzy from the lack of air. But hunger seemed to have taken the place of the anxiety she'd been suffering all evening. A hunger for him that was increasing with every sensual caress.

She wanted to meet his need, God help her. If she was totally honest she'd admit she wanted to give herself to him. She opened herself as she opened her mouth, letting his tongue tangle with hers and sweep all her doubts away.

Her knees were so weak that she was glad when his hands curved over her bottom. He caressed her boldly, his fingers invading the cleft between her cheeks. He was holding her tightly against him, and she felt his erection thrusting against her stomach.

The blood was now racing through her veins like liquid fire, the music playing in her ears like a plaintive song inside her head. Every nerve was acutely sensitive, feeding the needs he was inciting. She wanted him, she wanted his hands on her body. She wanted to be naked for him, she thought shamelessly. She wanted to feel his naked flesh against her skin.

When he bent lower and caught one taut nipple between his teeth, she almost went wild with longing. He sucked it strongly through the cloth, eliciting a moan of frustration from her lips. Looking down at his bent head, she couldn't prevent herself from touching him, feeling his sharp reaction under her palm.

Her free hand stroked his cheek, felt the faint roughness of his stubble beneath her touch. And when he released her breast she lifted his face to hers, initiating the kiss, cupping his face between her hands.

Her tongue darted to meet his and she heard his groan of pleasure. Then he took over, and she was helpless again beneath the eager, searching pressure of his mouth. Her head was spinning. She felt as if she was swimming in a rich dark sea of emotion. Yet she didn't—couldn't—think of drawing away.

The sensations that were governing her body were so delicious she couldn't deny them. Her breasts, her stomach, her abdomen, were sensitised to such an extent that she could do nothing but show him how she felt. She ached with feelings that compelled her to give in to him. She'd never experienced so much emotion in her life.

When he trailed hot kisses along her jawline to the quivering column of her throat she burrowed against him. They were still wearing their clothes and she wanted to be closer yet. She hardly hesitated before attempting to drag his shirt out of his pants. She wanted to feel his warm flesh beneath her hands.

But, as if that was the signal he had been waiting for, Alejandro stiffened. Expelling an uneven sigh, he lifted his head. His hands gripped her upper arms and he put her away from him. Holding her as she struggled to understand.

'I think not,' he said softly, as she swayed uncertainly before him. 'I think this is the moment when I say we have to talk.'

'To talk?' Abby tried to clear her head, but it wasn't easy. She blinked uncomprehendingly. 'I don't understand.'

'I think you do, *cara*,' he said, releasing her and moving across the cabin to pour himself more wine. 'I am only doing what you wanted. So talk to me, Abigail. Tell me why you think Edward is so keen for us to renew our—acquaintance.'

CHAPTER ELEVEN

ABBY shook her head, and then wished she hadn't. It just made her feel slightly sick and she prayed she wasn't about to throw up. That would be the last straw, she thought bitterly. The final humiliation. Somehow she had to deal with this with some dignity and pride.

But the rich food, the wine, dancing with Alejandro—especially dancing with Alejandro—had left her feeling dazed and vulnerable. And he knew it. That was why he was standing there, legs slightly apart, arms crossed over his midriff, the glass of red wine in his hand a scarlet stain against his white shirt. There was amusement in his face, too, she thought. A mocking acknowledgement of her weakness. Of how easy it had been to rob her of the veneer of indifference she'd attempted to display.

She wasn't displaying any indifference now. On the contrary, she knew she must look a total disaster. Her hair, unruly at the best of times, was wild about her shoulders, her shorts had been pushed low on her hips and her halter clung clammily to her breasts. She looked what she was: a woman who had been made mad, passionate love to. By a man who had deliberately robbed her of any self-respect...

She had to say something, she told herself urgently. She had to try and rescue the situation by showing him that she was above his petty sarcasm. It would be pointless to pretend that she hadn't been aroused by his lovemaking, but if she could convince him that she was no more ashamed of what had happened than he was, then she might stand a chance of saving face.

'I'm sorry,' she said at last, lifting both hands and sweeping her hair back from her face. She allowed her hands to rest at

112

the back of her neck, even though she knew it drew attention to the swollen fullness of her breasts and the betraying darkness on the cloth that his lips and tongue had made. 'I'm afraid I'd forgotten all about Eddie. Isn't that awful?' She forced a smile. 'Forgive me. What was it you were saying? Something about Eddie wanting us to get together?'

He was surprised. She could see that. And there was a faint trace of admiration in his eyes. He indicated the wine bottle beside him, offering her refreshment, but she wanted nothing else to impair her judgment tonight.

She moved her wrist in a negative gesture. She had to keep her head now, even if she had already proved how difficult that could be. And, groping behind her, she found the banquette, sinking down onto it with some relief.

'So,' she went on, not giving him the chance to take the initiative, 'perhaps you should tell me why you think that is.'

Alejandro lifted his glass to his lips before replying, and she had to steel herself not to watch the powerful muscles moving in his throat. Perhaps he needed the wine to give him courage, she thought without conviction. But surely what had happened hadn't all been on her side? He had been aroused. She was sure of it. And there'd been times when he'd seemed as much at the mercy of his senses as she was herself.

'*Bravo,*' he said now, putting down his empty glass and seating himself on the banquette opposite. 'You turn my words back on me in the hope that I will forget who started this— conversation, *no*?'

'*Well, I didn't start it,*' muttered Abby under her breath, relieved that he hadn't taken the seat beside her. But it wasn't all good news. Now he could look at her without obstruction. She felt as if she was in a spotlight, his dark eyes on her, narrowed and intent.

She licked her lips and tried to speak casually. 'I—I hoped you would tell me why you think Eddie is afraid,' she said evenly. She paused, and when he didn't answer her, she continued, 'You act like you have all the answers, but you don't explain what you mean.'

'Did I say I had all the answers?'

His brows arched interrogatively and she knew she was going to get no real explanations from him. The most she'd hoped for was that he might betray some titbit of information she could use to get her brother to confide in her. But Alejandro was giving nothing away.

Changing the subject, she said abruptly, 'What about the break-in at Eddie's apartment? I know you denied knowing anything about it when I mentioned it to Mrs Esquival, but we both know that wasn't what you said to me.'

'Do we?'

Once again he was deliberately obtuse, and she turned her head away from his bland look of enquiry. She could hardly believe that only a few minutes before they had been locked in each other's arms. She might still feel the shame of his lovemaking in her throbbing breast and in the burning and—oh, Lord—the *visible* scar on her neck, but he looked as cool and composed as ever. She could almost believe she'd imagined the whole thing.

Her eyes filled with tears and she had to blink hard to drive them away. She must not—*must not*—let him see that he had hurt as well as humiliated her. She might despise herself, but she refused to let him see it.

'So?' She had been silent too long, and he was waiting for her to answer him. 'Perhaps you should tell me what you feel about the break-in, *cara*. Do you think it was, as they say, some addict searching for money for a fix? Or was it—perhaps—a warning? Does your brother have enemies we know nothing about?'

He had her whole attention now, and she swiped the heels of her hands over her eyes before turning to look at him again. 'What enemies?' she echoed blankly, remembering the laptop computer lying untouched on the shelf.

'Who knows?' Again he drew back from telling her anything positive. 'But maybe it is time that you asked him.'

Abby swallowed. 'I'm asking you.'

'I know. But I cannot answer you.'

Abby shook her head. 'Can't or won't?' She sniffed. 'Are you sure you're not enjoying this?'

'Enjoying what?'

'This. Confusing me. Saying the robbery might be a warning.' Despite her best efforts, a tremor had entered her voice. 'Why can't you be honest with me for a change?'

'As you were with me?' he queried bleakly, and she gazed at him blankly.

'As I was with you?' she echoed. 'What are you talking about?'

'It is of no matter,' he replied, not pursuing it. He glanced behind him. 'Can I offer you some more wine?'

'I don't want anything. Only the truth,' she retorted unsteadily. Then, with determination, 'All right, if you won't tell me what you know about the break-in, perhaps you can tell me why Eddie and Lauren are having personal problems if they don't involve you? Eddie seems convinced she is seeing someone. Do you know if she is involved with someone else?'

Alejandro blew out a breath. 'Truly, you are *increíble, cara*. Why would you suppose that I would know this?'

'You are—close to her,' insisted Abby doggedly. 'She seems to trust you. If anyone knows what she's doing, it's you.'

'You flatter me.' Alejandro rose negligently to his feet. 'And even if it was true—and I am admitting nothing, you understand?—then you must know that I would respect her confidence in the same way as I respect yours.'

'Mine?' Abby said the word contemptuously, stung into retaliation. 'You've never shown me any respect. On the contrary. All you've ever done for me is ensure that I can never have—'

She broke off abruptly. Dear heaven, she'd almost said it. A sense of horror engulfed her at the realisation that she'd been in danger of betraying her deepest secret to him. The frustration she'd been feeling had briefly robbed her of her usual caution, and all the promises she'd made to herself while she'd been lying in her hospital bed had taken second place to the desire to wipe the smug complacency from his face.

She fought for control, aware that he was looking at her curiously now. The expression that had crossed her face, or perhaps the anguished sincerity in her voice, had alerted him to the fact that she had been about to deliver some telling news. He was obviously waiting for her to go on, but it would never happen, she assured herself sickly. He was never—*never*—going to find out what he'd done to her.

Feeling incredibly weak, she got unsteadily to her feet and said, 'I'd like to leave now.' She held up her head. 'Perhaps I could call a cab?'

'That will not be necessary.' Alejandro's eyes were narrowed. 'Carlos will take you.' He paused. 'But are you sure you want to go? You did not finish what you started to say.'

'It was of no importance,' she lied, aware that he didn't believe her. 'Actually, I'm not feeling very well. I'm sure you wouldn't want your friends to think you'd upset me.'

'Even if I have?' he countered, his tone betraying more warmth, as if he was feeling sorry for her, which she couldn't bear. 'I am sorry if I have disappointed you, Abigail. That was not my intention. But we are all human. And you are—you always were—a disturbingly attractive woman. I am afraid I let things go too far.'

'And you were always full of—' She bit off the word. 'Excuse me, Señor Varga, but I think I'm going to be sick.'

Of course she wasn't sick, even if her stomach was decidedly wobbly as Carlos drove her back to the Esquivals' villa.

'You all right, ma'am?' Carlos asked as he paused at the gates of the estate, and Abby wondered if he knew what was going on. Because Alejandro had bid her a polite, but definitely cool farewell, perhaps? The chauffeur must have noticed that his employer's attitude had been vastly different from the way he'd greeted her on her arrival. But had he also sensed the hostility that simmered between them? The awareness that held both distrust and suspicion?

She told herself she didn't care, and, forcing a small smile, she said, 'I'm fine, thank you. Just a little tired, that's all. You know how it is with jet lag.'

Carlos nodded, but she had the feeling he was far more astute than she was giving him credit for. 'I know how it is,' he conceded, and she had the bitter thought that this probably wasn't the first time he'd driven some pathetic woman home after Alejandro had discarded them. Someone had to do it, and his employer wouldn't do it himself.

To her relief, there was no sign of her hosts when she entered the villa. She thought she could hear the sound of voices and laughter from the patio, but she didn't stop to investigate. She remembered that the Esquivals had been expecting visitors that evening, and she had no desire to meet anyone else. She just wanted to go to bed and escape her thoughts in oblivion.

Informing the maid who had let her in that she was going to her room, she ran quickly up the stairs, not stopping until the door was closed behind her. She was making a habit of this, she thought miserably. Running away from her problems. Hiding in her room. And she had still to cope with the guilt she was feeling over betraying Ross. That ought to have been her main misgiving, but she couldn't deal with that tonight.

She knew Ross would be expecting her to call him. But there was no way she could come from Alejandro's arms and speak to her fiancé normally. He would hear the hesitation in her voice. What she'd done was unforgivable. And she didn't feel she could contemplate it.

Shedding the hateful shorts and halter, she went into her bathroom and stood for several minutes under a cool shower. She was trying to wash away the memory of Alejandro's hands upon her, trying to rid herself of the feeling that his fingerprints must still be visible on her skin.

As his teeth marks were visible on her neck, she acknowledged anxiously, seeing her reflection in the mirror and touching the bruised flesh with reluctant fingers. Dear Lord, why had he done it? Why had he branded her? Was it some sick way of showing her how helpless she was with him? Or was this Edward's answer? That he shouldn't send a woman to do a man's job?

Whatever his motives, she would have to hide it before she went down to breakfast in the morning. She could imagine Dolores's revulsion if she saw the mark. Not to mention Lauren and her brother. She had some elastic plasters in her toilet bag. She would have to use one of them.

It was after eleven by the time she crawled into bed, but she wasn't sleepy. She was tired, yes, but her mind was too active to allow her to sleep. The events of the evening kept going round and round in her head. Whatever way she looked at it, she had to admit that she had been as much to blame for what had happened as Alejandro.

Oh, he had instigated it, no doubt, by inviting her to dance, but he hadn't been totally responsible for what had come after. She'd wanted to dance with him. She'd wanted him to hold her, to kiss her, to *make love* to her. She'd been wholly at the mercy of her senses, and it was galling to realise that if he hadn't called a halt to what was happening, what had happened two years ago would have happened all over again.

But why? *Why?* Her eyes filled with tears. Was she so lacking in moral fibre that any man's embrace would have achieved the same result? No! It was Alejandro. It had always been Alejandro. He was like a fever in her blood, and, damn him, she didn't seem capable of putting him out of her mind…

Abby met Alejandro Varga for the first time just three days before her brother's wedding.

She'd arrived from England the day before, weary and jet lagged. It was the first time she'd travelled so far, and she was still slightly overwhelmed by the richness and beauty of her surroundings when she went down to the pool the next morning for a swim.

Mrs Esquival—there was no question of calling her Dolores in those days—had assured her she was welcome to treat the place as her home for the duration of her stay. Abby couldn't wait for Edward to arrive before taking advantage of the deliciously cool water.

Her brother was still living in the apartment he shared with two of the other chefs from the restaurant where he worked. And, although he'd put in an appearance the night before, it had been obvious to his sister that his association with the Esquivals was still very much that of employer and employee.

But meeting Lauren had been reassuring. She was evidently very much in love with her English fiancé. She'd greeted Abby like the sister she'd never had, asking her lots of questions about Edward's childhood, showing sympathy for the fact that Abby had virtually had to bring her brother up on her own. She'd thanked her, too, for allowing Edward to come to Florida, teasing him by speculating who she might have been marrying if he hadn't come to work for her father.

They'd seemed extremely happy together, and Abby, who had had some misgivings about the wedding, had been completely won over by Lauren's warmth and sincerity. For the first time in her life she felt that Edward was standing on his own two feet, and she was able to relax.

The plan was that Edward would come around this morning and take Abby sightseeing. But the pool was irresistible, and she'd swum several lengths before she realised that someone was standing on the tiled surround, watching her.

She thought at first that it was Edward. She came up, sweeping her hair from her eyes, prepared to make some teasing comment about him sleeping in as usual. Then she saw that it wasn't her brother, after all. The watcher was too tall, too dark, too overwhelmingly masculine to be mistaken for the younger man. Despite the heat, he was dressed in a charcoal-grey suit that fairly screamed its designer label, and, with his hands tucked casually into his trouser pockets, he looked both broodingly thoughtful and sexy as hell.

Abby's breath caught in the back of her throat as she struggled to put a name to the visitor. She'd met various members of Lauren's family the night before, but she was sure if she'd seen this man she'd have remembered. Though perhaps not.

She had been tired and there had been so many unfamiliar faces.

Whatever, she was at a disadvantage in the pool, and, wishing her swimsuit was more stylish than practical, she swam to the side where she'd left a towel and scrambled out. Then, wrapping the towel sarong-wise about her, she offered the man a tentative smile.

'I—it's a beautiful morning,' she said, groaning to find herself speaking about the weather. He would think that was all English people ever spoke about. 'I suppose you're used to it.'

The man inclined his head. 'I suppose I am,' he agreed, with a small smile that caused a ripple of awareness to feather down her spine. He had a faint accent, just as the Esquivals did, and there was an indulgent note in his voice as he added softly, 'You must be Edward's sister. Abigail, is it not?'

Abby swallowed. 'That's right.' She wasn't sure whether he expected them to shake hands and she made an awkward little move towards him. 'Um—have we met?'

'Regrettably, not until this moment,' he replied, solving her problem by closing the distance between them and bending to bestow a kiss on each cheek in turn. '*Bienvenido a* Miami, Abigail. I am happy to meet you.'

Abby gazed up at him for a moment, totally incapable of saying anything. She could still feel the brush of his lips on her cheek, the warmth of his breath against her skin. His response had been so swift, so unexpected, so totally earth-shattering, that she found herself speechless. And she was uneasily aware of a vulnerability she'd never felt before.

But she had to say something, and, taking a step back from him, she managed breathlessly, 'And you are...?'

'*Ah, perdón, cara,*' he exclaimed, his dark eyes alight with self-recrimination. '*Me olivido.* I forget. We have not been introduced. *No importa.* I am the cousin of Dolores, *sí*? Alejandro Varga. I am most happy to meet you, Abigail. We must see that you enjoy your visit to Florida. So much so that you will want to come back, *no*?'

'No. I mean, yes.' Abby was flustered. She realised the towel was slipping and hastily gathered it more closely about her. 'That is—I hope so.'

Alejandro smiled again and Abby felt a pleasurable pain in the pit of her stomach. But her face was hot and she was sure she must look like a ripe tomato.

'Good,' he said, and to her relief—or was it to her disappointment?—he made no further attempt to detain her. Instead, he stepped aside, allowing her free access to the steps that led up to the patio. 'I am sure we will meet again very soon,' he added as she reached the top of the steps. 'Until then, *adios*.'

'*Adi*—um—goodbye,' she mumbled foolishly, hardly knowing what she was saying. With a nervous backward glance she hurried into the house.

Of course she despised herself afterwards. She was sure he must have been amused by her complete lack of sophistication. It had only been his innate courtesy that had saved what had been for her a totally embarrassing encounter.

But that didn't stop her from wondering what he'd thought of her, from fretting over the way she'd reacted to what had actually been a perfectly normal introduction. He'd probably thought she wasn't used to talking to men. Which, unfortunately, was only too true. He might even have felt sorry for her. No, scrub that. He had definitely felt sorry for her. That was why he'd gone out of his way to put her at her ease.

But, heavens, he was so different from anyone she had ever dealt with, and she'd been hopelessly overwhelmed when she'd emerged from the water to find him watching her. Why had he been watching her? What possible interest could she have for him?

Despite his promises to take her sightseeing, Edward seemed more concerned with the final arrangements for his honeymoon than in making sure his sister was entertained. The Esquivals, naturally, were busy with the preparations for the wedding. Consequently, Abby found time lying heavily on her hands, and not even the delights of being able to swim and sunbathe if she wanted could entirely remove the suspicion that she was in the way.

There was so much going on around her: the house was rapidly filling with flowers, and marquee erectors and caterers were constantly on hand, discussing guest numbers and menus with Mrs Esquival. If Abby went down to the pool she had to run the gamut of a dozen pairs of dark eyes, and exposing her body to their evaluation became less and less appealing.

She had suggested that she might go out on her own, but Lauren's father had been unenthusiastic.

'You are a stranger here, Abigail,' he said on her second evening at dinner. 'You do not know your way about.' He looked at her brother then. 'Edward will look after you. You have some free time for your sister, *no*? You must make sure you do not neglect her, eh?'

Of course Edward would have promised his future father-in-law anything. But he had been absent for most of the day. He had said he would come round the following morning. But she was still waiting when Alejandro arrived.

The Cuban was dressed much less formally today, Abby noticed. Even so, his black tee shirt and drawstring khaki pants still looked expensive and elegant. But then, on him, anything would look good, she thought enviously. It was something to do with the almost graceful way he moved.

For once Dolores wasn't about, and he strolled onto the terrace with a cool familiarity. He smiled at the sight of Abby sitting on a lounge chair, an unopened book beside her. Her jean-clad knees were drawn up to her chin, and her arms were wrapped almost wistfully about them.

'All alone?' he remarked, startling her out of her reverie, and she immediately straightened her legs and ran a nervous hand over the curling halo of her hair.

'For now,' she agreed, glancing swiftly about her. 'Um— Mrs Esquival is somewhere around. Would you like me to get her for you?'

'No.' Alejandro raised his hand in a negative gesture when she would have scrambled off the lounger and gone looking for the other woman. 'I did not come here to interrupt Dolores. I am sure she has enough to do as it is. If I know my cousin, everything will have to adhere to her most exacting standards. The bride, the flowers, the service; even the cake must not be less than perfect, *no*?'

'No.' Abby felt a smile tilt the corners of her mouth. He was obviously amused, too, and he didn't hide it. His eyes glinted with a rueful humour that she could share.

'So, what have you planned for the rest of the day?' he enquired, seating himself on the side of the lounger nearest to her. He arched a dark brow. 'Your brother is taking you sight-seeing, perhaps?'

'I don't know what Eddie's doing,' she replied, unable to keep the disappointment out of her voice. 'I've hardly seen him since I arrived.'

'No?' Alejandro frowned. 'But surely yesterday—?'

'He arrived in time for dinner,' said Abby, and then, feeling slightly disloyal for talking about her brother in this way, she added quickly, 'He has a lot to do, too. He and Lauren are going to Bali for their honeymoon, as you probably know, and he wants to make sure everything goes smoothly. He wants no hang-ups over passports or accommodation, that sort of thing.'

Alejandro was silent for a moment, and then he said quietly, 'I would have thought such details could be safely left in the hands of his travel agent, but who knows? Edward may be like Dolores. I know she worries too much.'

Abby had the feeling that Edward was nothing like his future mother-in-law. He'd never worried about anything in his life. But she didn't say so. This man was a stranger to her, after all. Just because he was a cousin of Dolores that did not give her a reason to confide in him.

'*Bien.*' He seemed to come to a decision. 'Then perhaps you will permit me to give you a guided tour of the city, *no*? I do not promise to know everything about it. I was born in Havana, *por supuesto*. But I have lived here for over twenty years, and I have come to regard the city as my home.'

Abby's face flamed. 'Oh—but that's not necessary,' she began, sure now that he was feeling sorry for her. 'I mean—I can wait—'

'For Edward?' suggested Alejandro drily. 'Yes, you can. But I am here and I am more than willing to offer myself as your escort.' His dark eyes searched her face. 'What do you say?'

What could she say? What *should* she say? she asked herself a little breathlessly. She wanted to go. Of course she did. But should she? Would Edward approve?

Did she care?

'I—it's very kind of you,' she murmured. 'If Dolores doesn't need my help—'

'You will come?'

Abby took a breath. 'All right,' she said weakly. Then, glancing at her jeans, 'But I'll have to change first.'

'Very well.'

Alejandro inclined his head, getting to his feet as she did, and for a heart-stopping moment he was close enough for her to feel the heat of his muscled frame. His arm touched her breast as he turned away, and, hearing her sudden intake of air, he turned towards her.

'I am sorry,' he said softly. 'I am clumsy. Are you hurt?'

'No. No, not at all,' she assured him urgently, putting the width of the terrace between them. If she felt any discomfort it was not because of the disturbing brush of his hand. 'I—I'll get changed. I won't be long.'

CHAPTER TWELVE

ABBY took a few minutes to sluice her hot face with cold water, but it did no good. When she gazed at her reflection in the bathroom mirror her cheeks were still bright with colour. But what could she expect? It wasn't every day that she was invited to go sightseeing with an attractive man like Alejandro Varga. And, whether he felt sorry for her or not, she owed it to herself to enjoy the experience.

Fortunately, she'd brought some pretty outfits with her, imagining that Edward would be only too eager to show her where he lived and how familiar with the city he was. But then, she'd also expected to stay with him, not with his future in-laws, and she wasn't entirely sure that accepting Alejandro's invitation would meet with universal approval.

Dismissing such negative thoughts, she chose a simple cream dress with an embroidered hem. Its draped bodice exposed the dusky hollow of her cleavage and its short skirt complemented her long shapely legs.

No one could ever accuse her of being thin, she thought ruefully, turning sideways in front of the mirror. But she was slim in all the right places, and with her hair controlled by two narrow braids at each temple she had infinitely more confidence in herself. She was still flushed, of course, but she couldn't help that. At least the cream dress didn't clash with her fiery hair.

Slipping slingbacks that added an extra couple of inches to her height onto her feet, she left her room and went back downstairs. And knew, as soon as she saw Alejandro waiting in the marble entry, that he thought she had made the right choice.

'I have told Dolores you are going out,' he said at once,

forestalling her intention of going to speak to her hostess. Hi
eyes assessed her appearance with evident approval. 'You look
delightful, *cara*. Come. My car is just outside.'

'But what about Lauren?'

'I'm told that Lauren is having a final fitting at the dress
maker's,' Alejandro informed her smoothly, urging her to
wards the door. He cast a faintly impatient glance at the hov
ering maid. 'Tell your mistress the young lady will be back
after lunch, *por favor*.'

'Oughtn't I to say goodbye to Dolores?' Abby persisted
and Alejandro gave a mocking smile.

'So long as you are aware that she may feel obligated to
act as chaperon,' he remarked drily 'She probably thinks your
brother is going with us. I have said nothing to disabuse her
of the thought.'

'Well…' Abby murmured weakly, aware that she was prob
ably taking an enormous risk by going out with him alone
'All right.' She stepped out into the bright sunlight. 'What a
beautiful morning! It is a shame to stay in the house.'

Alejandro inclined his head, going past her to swing open
the nearside door of the sleek black limousine that was parked
at the foot of the steps. Then, after helping her inside, where
the feel of cool soft leather and the pleasurable aromas of
expensive soap and clean male skin assaulted her senses, he
walked round the bonnet and coiled his length beside her.

The look he gave her then mingled warm admiration with
satisfaction, and she realised once again that he had probably
known she'd give in all along. 'If you will forgive the pre
sumption, I prefer there to be no extraneous distractions,' he
remarked, starting the engine of the powerful vehicle. 'You
will forgive me for wanting you to myself.'

Abby shook her head. She didn't really believe him, but she
had the feeling it would be better if she didn't probe too deeply
into his motivations. One way or another, she was committed
to spending the morning with him. If Dolores didn't approve
she would get over it. She would just have to face the con
sequences when she got back.

They drove first to Miami Beach, crossing one of the many causeways that linked the long strip of land, famous for its many fabulous hotels, from the mainland. Abby found the trip along Collins Avenue a revelation. Each glass and steel monolith seemed to be trying to outdo its neighbour, with the art deco hotels of Ocean Drive monuments to its colourful history.

Alejandro parked the car and they walked past the bars and sidewalk cafés that spilled from hotel patios all along the boulevard. He explained that the area had undergone a complete renovation in recent years, and that it was very much a going place after dark. But he also showed her the mansion where a famous dress designer had been murdered on his own doorstep, and took her for coffee at the News Café, which was already packed with residents and tourists eager for the latest gossip.

Later, they drove into the city itself, and Abby was amazed to see what a mixture of styles and cultures it was. Skyscrapers stood cheek by jowl with tacky discount stores, and many of the shops catered to a mainly South American clientele.

Once again Alejandro parked the car in one of the secure lots, and, after assuring himself that she was happy to walk, he took her on a tour of some of Miami's more impressive tourist establishments. Flagler Street was home to two of southern Florida's more famous museums, one of which was an art museum which Abby loved. A visitors' gallery provided lots of ways to research the paintings being exhibited and she wished museums back home were more visitor-friendly like this.

Alejandro also showed her a part of Biscayne Boulevard that was more continental than anything she had seen so far. Then he took her for lunch at the top of one of the tallest buildings in the city. The view across the bay was stunning, blue skies and sunlit water providing a vista she thought she'd never forget.

Abby was so glad she hadn't allowed her innate cautiousness to deter her from spending this time with Alejandro. He had been a marvellous guide, both interesting and knowledgeable, and she was sure she'd learned more in the past few hours than she would ever have thought possible. She already felt more at home here and, although she had listened to his warning about taking safety for granted, she had been given an unforgettable taste of the real Miami.

Not surprisingly, Alejandro offered to choose what they had for lunch also. And, after dining on broiled shrimp and tangy cheese and fresh fruit salad, Abby was glad she'd taken his advice. She'd never eaten such tasty shellfish, or gorged on such juicy pineapple and melon. There was papaya, too, its orange flesh sweet and luscious, and slices of avocado, sharp with a lemon dressing.

Although they'd conducted a desultory conversation throughout the meal, it wasn't until rich dark coffee had been served that Alejandro asked her if she had enjoyed herself.

'Need you ask?' Abby was amazed that he should have any doubts. But, meeting his dark eyes across the suddenly narrow width of the table, she was immediately aware of the intimacy of his question. Yet, determined not to back down, she countered daringly, 'Have you?'

Alejandro's lips tilted. 'What was it you said?' he murmured. 'Need you ask?' His smile deepened. 'But, yes, I have enjoyed myself very much, *cara*. You are a—how shall I put it?—a delightful companion.'

'A naïve one,' said Abby ruefully, guessing he would never be anything but polite. 'But I am grateful to you for taking the time to—'

'No.' His sudden interjection caused her to break off in mid sentence. 'Do not say it, *cara*. Your gratitude is not necessary. Not necessary at all. Spending the morning with you has been a pleasure. I am lucky to have been honoured with the experience.'

Abby smiled then. She couldn't help herself. He was so charming! He always said the right thing. But, while she appreciated his kindness, she couldn't help wishing she was the kind of woman who took his brand of flattery for granted.

'You're a nice man, Mr Varga,' she said, not knowing what

o say. She put down her coffee cup and linked her fingers on
he table. 'But I'm sure you have more important things to do
han take me sightseeing.'

Alejandro shrugged. 'And if I tell you that I do not? What
hen?'

A trace of colour invaded her cheeks. 'I'd say you were
being polite—but not entirely truthful.'

'No?'

'No.' She sighed, spreading one hand expressively. 'You're
Dolores's cousin, right?' And, at his nod, 'You arrived this
morning—as you did yesterday morning,' she reminded him
nervously, 'and found me on my own again. I'd say you felt
sorry for me. That was why you asked me out.'

Alejandro lay back in his chair. 'Is that the impression I
have given you?'

'No.' Abby had to be honest. 'But sightseeing can be bor-
ing. Particularly if you've seen it all before. Eddie hates looking round museums. I have to admit he's not much interested
in the past.'

'So—I have saved your brother from a fate worse than
death, hmm?' he remarked drily, and she had to smile again.

'I suppose,' she murmured ruefully. 'Whatever, I know he'll
be grateful to you for looking after me as you have.'

'You think so?'

'I know so,' she assured him fervently, hoping Edward
would agree. 'Um—do you know my brother well?'

'I have met him,' said Alejandro non-committally. 'I understand he works for Luis in one of his restaurants, *no*?'

'That's right.' Abby nodded. 'That was how he met Lauren.
He came to work in America two years ago.'

'Ah.' Alejandro absorbed this. 'But you are the only member of his family coming for the wedding, *sí*?'

'Yes.' Abby loved the way he interspersed his sentences
with Spanish words and phrases. 'Actually, apart from some
distant cousins, there is no one else. Our father—died some
years ago.'

'And your mother also?'

'Well—no.' Abby hesitated. 'Our mother left when Eddie and I were just children. We haven't seen her since.'

'*Lo entiendo.*' Alejandro saw her confusion and added swiftly, 'I understand.' He frowned. 'But you must have been devastated when your brother left England. Did you never consider accompanying him?'

'Oh, no.' Abby spoke without thinking. 'I wouldn't have wanted to cramp his style.'

'To cramp his style?' echoed Alejandro curiously, and Abby sighed.

'Well, yes,' she responded lamely. 'That is—Eddie had a job waiting for him and I—I didn't.'

She could hardly tell this man about Edward's infatuation with Selina Steward. Not when she was here to attend his wedding to someone else.

'I see.' Alejandro nodded, and although Abby knew he couldn't possibly know what she was thinking she had the uneasy feeling that he did. 'And do you work in the restaurant business also?'

'I'm a teacher,' said Abby at once, feeling on safer ground. 'An English teacher.' She pulled a wry face. 'Not half as glamorous, I'm afraid.'

'That depends on your point of view,' remarked her companion easily. 'Not everyone who works in the restaurant business is involved in the preparation of the food, *tu sabes.*'

'No.' Abby conceded his point. Then, deciding they had talked enough about her, she ventured, 'And you, Mr Varga? Are you involved in the restaurant business yourself?'

'Not directly,' he replied, his dark eyes disturbingly indulgent. 'I do many things, Abigail. Not all of them either glamorous or interesting.'

'I'm sure that's not true.' Abby's tongue circled her upper lip. 'But you weren't born here, you said?' she persisted. 'Does—er—does the rest of your family still live in Cuba?'

He was quiet for so long she thought at first he wasn't going to answer her. But then he shifted in his seat and said, 'I have relatives who still live in the old country, it is true. Aunts, uncles, cousins—many of whom would never dream of leaving their homeland. But I have relatives here, too. When my grandfather moved his family to the United States my father and mother came with him.'

'And your mother didn't mind?' Abby asked. 'Leaving her own family behind?'

'Ah, no.' Alejandro straightened, resting one elbow on the table. 'You do not understand, *cara*. My mother was an American.'

'Oh.' Abby supposed that explained why he possessed such an attractive mix of Spanish gallantry and American sophistication. She hesitated a moment, and then said a little daringly, 'So—how did they meet?'

'You mean, because of the hostilities that have existed between this country and Cuba for so many years?' he queried softly, and she nodded. '*Sí*, you might think it was an unlikely union, eh?'

'I was curious, that's all.' Abby felt embarrassed. 'But if you'd rather not talk about it—'

'Not at all.' He shrugged, his powerful shoulders moving easily beneath his silk jacket. 'My mother was a nurse. She had been working in Cuba prior to the revolution, and regrettably she was caught up in the civil war that devastated the country. She was given refuge by my father's family and she and my father fell in love. They were married in 1960, just as the US government declared an economic embargo. I was born the following year.'

Abby was intrigued. 'What a wonderful story.'

'You think?' Alejandro paused. 'Well, they loved one another, that is true. But because of land reform, and the fact that my grandfather was unable to sell his sugar cane to the United States, they were eventually forced to leave. We were virtually penniless when we arrived in Florida. But my grandfather was an enterprising man and he invested what little money he had in the leisure and tourism industry. By the time my father took over the business it was a much bigger concern, and I—' He pulled a wry face. 'I have been lucky.'

Abby doubted luck had much to do with it. Alejandro struck her as being a very astute individual himself. But she didn' want to press him, so instead she said, 'Are your grandparent: still alive?'

'Regrettably, no.' Alejandro shook his head. 'My father is *por supuesto*. But my mother died five years ago.'

Abby was sympathetic. 'Do you have brothers and sisters? 'Two brothers, three sisters.' He smiled mockingly. 'Cuban: usually have large families. But only my oldest sister still live: in Florida. The rest are married and scattered about the coun try.'

'But you see them often?' suggested Abby, thinking how nice it must be to have a large family. 'I hope Eddie and Lauren go ahead and have children. I can't wait to become ar aunt myself.'

'Or a mother?' remarked Alejandro seductively. 'Surely you wish to have children of your own?'

'Well, of course I do,' Abby exclaimed, feeling her face heating again. 'But I'm not on the point of getting married Eddie is.'

'You do not have to be married to have children,' pointed out Alejandro drily, and Abby quivered at the images his words created. A vision of herself pregnant with his chilc flashed before her eyes and she hurriedly addressed herself tc her coffee again to avoid his knowing gaze.

'Well, as I'm not involved with anyone at the moment, the question doesn't arise,' she mumbled into her cup. 'Um— think I ought to be getting back, don't you?'

Contrary to what Alejandro had told her, Mrs Esquival wasn' at all pleased to hear where Abby had been and who she had been with. Apparently Alejandro had given Dolores the im pression that he'd arranged for her guest to join a sightseeing tour—which was probably why he'd balked Abby's efforts tc speak to the other woman before they left. He'd said nothing about escorting her himself, and it was obvious that Lauren': mother thought Abby had taken advantage of his kindness.

Abby went from feeling guilty to harbouring a certain resentment towards the older woman. It wasn't as if Alejandro was complaining, and she certainly hadn't asked him to take her out. Consequently, when he rang her the following morning and offered to take her to dinner at a famous South Beach restaurant that evening, she didn't hesitate before accepting his invitation.

Why shouldn't she have some fun while she was here? she defended herself. It wasn't as if Edward was falling over himself to look after her. And, although the Esquivals were polite, she never felt anything but a guest in their home.

The evening was every bit as exciting as she'd anticipated. This time there was no avoiding Dolores's disapproval, but Alejandro seemed indifferent to his cousin's displeasure. When she suggested that perhaps Abby ought to be resting, in preparation for the following evening's festivities, he merely pulled a wry face and said, 'I am sure Abigail will have plenty of time to relax tomorrow, *querida*. And, as you appear to have everything under control, why should she not enjoy herself?'

'People will talk,' Dolores exclaimed tersely, but Alejandro's face only stiffened into a sardonic smile.

'Let them,' he remarked, ushering his companion towards the door. '*Adios*, Luis. I promise I will return your guest safely to you.'

They started the evening at a flashy bar on Ocean Drive, rubbing shoulders with several famous Hollywood faces who seemed to be enjoying their celebrity status. Abby was sure Alejandro had only taken her there to see the wide-eyed bemusement on her face, and she wasn't at all surprised when he took her somewhere much more exclusive for dinner.

The food had a West Indian bias this time, and Abby enjoyed the subtle blends of herbs and spices that flavoured the many exotic dishes she was offered. Afterwards, they strolled along the sidewalk, taking in the culture overload that was South Beach, and Abby caught her breath when he took her hand and linked his fingers with hers.

Although she'd sensed that he seemed to find her particularly attractive this evening, she was totally unprepared when he backed her into a shadowy doorway between two hotels and kissed her. The fire that leapt between them startled him, too, she thought, and he repeated the kiss, this time parting her lips with his tongue and thrusting his way into her mouth.

He whispered to her in his own language, low, husky sounds that made her feel weak at the knees. Cupping her head in one large hand, he angled her face so that he could go on kissing her, drinking from her lips, reducing her to a trembling mass of shivering anticipation.

She had never had such feelings before. She'd been kissed before; of course she had. But the men she'd dated had never made her feel like this, had never aroused the needs that were now churning inside her.

Almost without thinking, she lifted her hands to his shoulders, gripping the satin lapels of his tuxedo, trying to anchor herself in a world that was suddenly out of control. The crowds about them disappeared, the sounds and the music fading into nothingness as she drowned in the sensuous ardour of his touch. She felt his hands at her waist, felt them brush too briefly over the rounded curve of her bottom, and arched against him. And felt the unmistakable ridge of his arousal hard between them.

'Cara.' His voice was thick with emotion, but although she wanted to protest she sensed his withdrawal. 'No ahora,' he whispered ruefully. 'Not here. Not now.' His thumb brushed across her soft mouth, parting her lips almost roughly. 'Tomorrow, hmm? We will continue this tomorrow. After the wedding, no? We will go somewhere where we can be alone.'

Of course she told herself that nothing more would come of it. The things he'd said had been spoken in the heat of the moment, and once he had had time to think about it he'd realise that they had nothing in common. Except a mutual desire to tear one another's clothes off, she thought, quivering as she lay in bed that night. And how sensible was that?

But she feared sense had little to do with it.

The wedding took place in the late afternoon. Lauren made a beautiful bride, and Abby had never been so proud of her brother as she was when he stood at his wife's side welcoming their guests.

As Alejandro had teased, Dolores had left nothing to chance, and every detail of the ceremony and the reception that followed it had been organised in every detail. A twenty-four-piece orchestra played while the guests dined on steak and shellfish, strawberries and champagne. A veritable swarm of waiters kept glasses filled and offered trays of seafood delicacies, chicken *vol-au-vents*, mounds of caviar. Ice sculptures melted in the early-evening heat, and jackets were shed as the bride and groom shared a romantic waltz before going to prepare for their departure.

After they had left for the airport Abby, who had felt very much the outsider for most of the afternoon, eased her feet out of her high heels and sought the comparative coolness of the loggia. She was glad everything had gone so well, but she was also glad it was over. The Esquivals' friends and relations were almost all of Cuban descent, and she had little in common with them.

All except Alejandro, she thought, finding a lounge chair and stretching her toes with some relief. But then, Lauren's mother had ensured that he had no time to waste on their annoying little English guest. Dolores had spent most of the reception hanging onto his arm and Alejandro had been too polite—or too relieved at having the initiative snatched away from him—to do anything about it.

'So this is where you are hiding yourself.'

His voice came out of the darkness. Although the rest of the garden was floodlit for the occasion, the servants had extinguished many of the lamps around the house. In consequence, Alejandro was in shadow. Until he moved closer and she could see his face.

'I—I was just resting my feet,' she said awkwardly, wondering if she could slip her shoes on without him noticing. 'It's been a long evening.'

'But a very successful one,' remarked Alejandro, moving her feet aside to sit on the end of her chair. His hands lingered on her instep, his fingers searching for and finding the aching pads beneath her toes. 'Your brother and his new wife looked suitably virginal, did you not think so? It is amazing what an occasion like this can do.'

Abby swallowed. 'It was a wonderful wedding,' she agreed. Then, with some embarrassment, 'You don't have to do that, you know.'

'But you are enjoying it, *sí*,' he murmured, his fingers miraculously massaging her aches and pains away. '*Lo importante*, you are enjoying it, *no*? I know you are. Your eyes betray you.'

'All the same...' Abby made a helpless gesture. 'Shouldn't you be with the other guests? The dancing has started. I'm sure Dolores will be looking for you.'

'I have done my duty, *cara*,' he told her softly. 'The bride and groom have departed and the rest of the evening is mine. *Ours*,' he corrected himself, his fingers circling her ankle possessively. 'Come, *cara*. I want to take you for a drive.'

Abby knew she should demur. She knew perfectly well that Dolores would not approve, and as she was leaving for home the next day she should be doing her packing. But her host and hostess were busy with their guests and no one noticed them leaving. Feeling like a thief, she allowed Alejandro to whisk her away in his convertible, the night air cooling her temples but making little impact on her blood.

They drove for a while along the coastal highway, and the breeze off the ocean made a tangle of her hair. She'd secured it in a French twist for the wedding, the formal style had seemed more suitable for the occasion, but now she gave up any hope of rescuing the fiery strands that blew about her face. Besides, she had the feeling that Alejandro preferred her hair loose, despite its wildness. His arm was along the back of her seat and his fingers caressed her nape, dislodging the few clips that still remained.

They eventually turned away from the water, threading their

way through wide streets with gabled houses that had given this area of Miami its name. Street lamps illuminated pastel-shaded houses and parks where fountains played. But the most memorable thing of all was the lush vegetation, and the exciting scents of the flowers on display.

The house Alejandro took her to was on Old Okra Road, an impressive Spanish-style dwelling, set behind towering oaks and stucco walls. A servant admitted them and then, on Alejandro's orders, left them to themselves, allowing him to show her round his home.

The things Abby remembered afterwards were the huge fireplace that took up almost the whole of one wall in the drawing room, decorated with Italian tile, and the massive oval swimming pool that was lit from below and gleamed with a turquoise beauty in the darkness. She also remembered the master bedroom suite and the enormous square bed that adorned it.

Alejandro poured them both a glass of wine and then opened the sliding doors onto the patio. They stepped outside with their drinks and Abby expressed her delight at the sight of the pool. 'You're so lucky,' she said. 'In this climate I expect you can swim all the year round. Apart from the fact that few people have pools back home, there are only a few months in the year when it's warm enough to use them.'

Alejandro shrugged. 'We have our cold days, too,' he said drily. 'And just occasionally a hurricane comes along to—how do you say it?—to keep us on our toes, *no*?' He smiled. 'You like to swim?'

Abby glanced up at him for a moment and then took a sip of her wine. 'Very much,' she said, wondering if he was remembering how they had met.

'Then perhaps we should,' murmured Alejandro softly. 'What do you think? It is warm enough, *desde luego*. And I can recommend it.'

Abby's jaw dropped. 'What? Now?'

'Why not?' His dark gaze seemed to caress her. 'Have you never gone swimming after dark?'

'Only—only in a hotel pool,' she admitted after a moment.

'When a girlfriend and I went on holiday to France. But lots of people were in the pool at the time. It was a sort of evening pool-party-cum-barbecue, you see.'

'Ah.' Alejandro inclined his head. 'So—shall we?'

Abby shook her head. 'I don't have anything to wear.'

'Why wear anything?' asked Alejandro, his fingertips tracing the soft contours of her arm. 'In this country we call it skinny-dipping. It is much more fun to swim without clothes.'

Abby was sure it was. She was also sure he was probably experienced at it. But she wasn't. She'd never taken her clothes off in front of a man before. The very idea was daunting.

'I—don't think—' she was beginning, when he set down his glass and started to unfasten his dinner jacket. Depositing it on the nearby swing-seat, he tackled the buttons on his shirt, tossing his tie aside as he did so.

Beneath his shirt, his skin was darkly tanned and roughened by a mat of dark hair. The hair was thickest between his nipples and arrowed down to his navel. Abby dragged her eyes away when his hand moved to the buckle of his belt.

With his belt hanging loose and the waistband of his trousers unfastened he stood before her, and Abby's mouth dried at the realisation that he intended to go the whole way. 'Do not be afraid, *cara*,' he said softly. 'I will not hurt you. I just want you to enjoy yourself, to cast off these inhibitions that are stopping you from having fun.'

Abby shook her head. 'I can't,' she said, emptying her glass in one unladylike gulp and turning away. 'If you want to swim, go ahead. I—I'll wait for you in the house.'

'*Pobrecita,*' he whispered huskily, and when she would have put the width of the patio between them he caught her from behind, his arm strong about her waist. 'Such a *timido* little one,' he added, drawing her back against his powerful frame. 'Have I embarrassed you again? Would you not like to cool off in the water?'

Abby could think of nothing she'd like more—if she wasn't

so nervous about taking off her clothes. But it was no good. She couldn't do it. However tempting the prospect might be.

'I'm—I'm sure it would be delightful,' she said honestly. 'But we hardly know one another. I couldn't—'

'Okay.' Without another word he released her. And as Abby hovered uncertainly by the glass doors, not sure how—or even if—she should proceed, she heard a sudden splash behind her and realised Alejandro had dived into the pool.

She turned then, unable to prevent herself, and was just in time to see Alejandro's dark head appear above the water. He swept back his hair with a careless hand and then grinned in a way that sent a coil of heat into the pit of her stomach. *'Dios,'* he said ruefully, 'I am not in good shape. I must start taking regular exercise again.'

Abby thought that was something of an exaggeration. From what she'd seen, Alejandro was in very good shape indeed. All he was trying to do was make her feel better about herself. Perhaps he suspected that the real reason she hadn't accepted his invitation was because she was intensely conscious of being several pounds overweight.

'Is the water cold?' she asked, unable to force herself to leave him and go into the house.

'Try it,' he said, and she stepped forward and squatted down on the tiled surround. She dipped her hand into the water and found it wasn't cold at all, just soft and inviting. How she wished she had the guts to join him. This might be her only chance to swim in the nude.

But such thoughts seemed a betrayal of all she'd ever tried to teach her brother. Abby straightened, and Alejandro swam to the side to look up at her with an enquiring gaze. 'What are you afraid of, *cara*?' he asked. 'I promise I will keep my distance. I will even allow you to keep on your underwear, if that will satisfy your modest little soul.'

Abby expelled a breath, remembering that her underwear was barely worthy of the name. Her cream lace bra and matching panties had been designed with tantalisation in mind, not modesty. She had the feeling she'd feel more exposed in them than in her bare skin.

'You don't understand,' she said at last, her breasts rising and falling rapidly with the agitation she was feeling. 'I'm not like you, Alejandro. I'm not used to getting undressed in front of strangers.'

'And you think I am?' he queried gently. '*Querida*, I thought I was making it easier for you. Contrary to your suspicions, I do not make a habit of taking my clothes off in public. But we are alone here. There are no eyes watching us. No eyes watching *you*. Only mine.'

And that was what she was afraid of.

And yet...

What did she really have to lose? she asked herself. She wasn't a virgin. True, her only experience of sex had been in the back seat of a car, and that had ended almost as soon as it had begun. But she wasn't afraid. Only afraid of getting hurt—emotionally hurt, she acknowledged unhappily. Alejandro Varga was like no man she had ever known. And in a few short days he had unknowingly captured her heart.

CHAPTER THIRTEEN

As IF abandoning any further attempt to persuade her, Alejandro turned and swam leisurely away from her. The movement caused the water to ripple along the edge of the pool below her, fragmenting the underwater lighting like shards of glass. And exposing the paler shade of his buttocks, taut and firm beneath the surface.

Abby sucked in a breath and, unable to stop herself, she took one foot out of her shoe and tested the temperature of the water again. As before, it felt lukewarm, still retaining the heat from that day's sun. Without giving herself time to have second thoughts, she stepped out of her shoes and unbuttoned the ice-green jacket of her two-piece. Shedding it onto the tiled surround, she dropped her skirt, too, and quickly slipped into the water.

Despite its apparent warmth, that initial plunge almost took her breath away. But she didn't think about that. Didn't think about anything—particularly not Alejandro. Kicking away from the side, she swam smoothly across the pool.

She was aware that Alejandro must have felt the movement in the water, but she didn't allow herself to speculate on what might happen now. This was her last night in Miami; her last chance to do something reckless. Tomorrow she would be sane and sensible again. And what could be more sane and sensible than getting on the plane back home?

The pool was perhaps five feet in depth around the rim, but it swiftly sloped away to deeper water. It was long, too, easily seventy-five feet, surrounded at the far end by lush greenery, the petals of a magnolia floating like stars upon the water.

When Alejandro surfaced some six feet away from where she was standing she couldn't prevent one hand from spreading almost protectively across her chest. She was uneasily aware that her bra and panties were virtually transparent now that they were wet, and looked just as provocatively suggestive as she'd imagined.

'You changed your mind,' he said, not coming any closer, and she wondered if that was for her benefit or his. Beneath the surface his skin gleamed darkly, and she had to force herself not to speculate about what she couldn't see.

'I was hot,' she said, as if that was an answer. 'You don't mind, do you?' Which was a ridiculous question to ask.

'Why should I mind?' he queried, his lips tilting humorously. 'You are free to do what you like in my home.' But his eyes darkened as he looked at her, and she was suddenly aware of how impulsive she'd been in taking off her clothes.

'It's a big pool,' she said foolishly, desperate to say something, *anything*, to deflect the deepening awareness between them, and he shook his head, flicking droplets of water in all directions.

'Size is not everything,' he remarked drily. 'I believe that is what they say. Personally, I think it depends what you are talking about, *no*?'

Abby felt her face grow warm with colour. Although he wasn't touching her, his words brushed seductively across her skin. It was so easy for him to embarrass her. She'd never met anyone who played these verbal games so well.

'Well, I think it's a big pool,' she insisted, trying to ignore his amusement. 'It's bigger than the one at the Esquivals', anyway. And deeper, too, I should imagine. How deep is it, actually?'

Alejandro's mouth compressed for a moment, and then, to her dismay, he swam lazily across the space between them. 'The pool is twenty-five metres in length, and it is four metres at its deepest point,' he told her solemnly. His feet touched the tiles as he straightened. 'And I know what you are trying to do.'

Abby recoiled, but with the edge of the pool at her back she didn't have far to go. 'I'm trying to show an interest in my surroundings,' she replied defensively. 'You may be used to—to all this, but I'm not.'

Alejandro put one hand on the rim at either side of her, successfully imprisoning her within the circle of his arms. 'No,' he said softly, his eyes warm and invasive, 'you are trying to distract me. You think if you babble on about the pool and its size I will forget the reason why I brought you here.' His gaze dropped to the revealing cleavage of her bra, where her treacherous nipples strained against the lace. '*Ni hablar, cara.* No way. I am a man, and I would not be human if I did not want to make love to you.'

Abby tried to keep calm. 'I thought you invited me to swim in the pool,' she said, resisting the urge she had to try and cover herself. 'That's why I'm here, anyway.'

'*Ah, cara…*' His lips twisted. 'I did not know you could be such a liar.' One hand moved and curved knowingly about her nape, his thumb catching in the gold hoop she wore in her ear and tugging almost cruelly. 'Do you not know that your body is betraying you? That it is almost as eager as I to cast off these—' one finger slid the strap of her bra off her shoulder '—these unnecessary sops to your conscience, *no*?'

Abby's fingers moved to restore the strap to her shoulder, but Alejandro was quicker. With ruthless efficiency his hand dipped behind her back and unfastened the clasp, so that her breasts tumbled free of the confining lace.

That was too much. 'Don't!' she exclaimed in a panicked voice. 'You're wrong about me. I didn't come here to—to sleep with you. I—don't do things like that.'

'Who said anything about sleeping?' countered Alejandro, lowering his head and covering her anxious lips with his. The hair on his chest brushed provocatively against her nipples and her breath caught in her throat. '*Ah, querida, te deseo.* I want you. *Besame, cara.* Kiss me. *Quiero hacerte el amor.*'

Abby felt the weakness of her own defences. The reality of his nude body against hers was more sensual than she had ever dreamed. Around them, the water ebbed and flowed, sensitising her skin in ways she had never known before. Its coolness lapped like silk about her shoulders, moving as he was moving, letting her feel the heat that their bodies were creating. When he tossed her bra onto the side she was almost grateful for the freedom it gave her.

Then his lips were on hers again, his tongue slipping between her teeth and making its own possession. The kiss deepened, lengthened, robbed her of breath so that she could only cling to his arms for support. Hot and unashamedly sexual, his mouth plundered hers hungrily, his tongue invading and retreating in a dance as old as time.

Abby was incapable of resisting him. She felt his hands beneath the water, shaping the curve of her waist, caressing the rounded swell of her bottom. She was suddenly desperate to be free of the scrap of lace that prevented him from touching her there, and when Alejandro found the high leg of her panties and probed beneath she whimpered. The wet petals spread eagerly to admit his searching fingers and a pulse beat hotly between her legs.

'Oh, my God,' she groaned shakily, unable to prevent herself from crying out, and Alejandro's face filled with satisfaction as he pressed the offending garment down her legs.

'Better?' he asked huskily, the throbbing heat of his arousal nudging her mound. And when she could only nod her agreement, he tucked his hands beneath her bottom and lifted her against him.

Abby wound her legs about his waist, but although it pleased her to feel his erection touching her aching core, it was not what Alejandro wanted.

'Not here,' he said. 'Not like this, *cara*. I want to love you, Abigail. But I want to lay you on my bed, to look at you, to show how much I want you.'

At that moment Abby thought she would have been content if he'd pushed his way inside her there and then. She'd never felt this desire for a man before, and the needs he'd inspired inside her—had been inspiring inside her, actually, since they'd first met—demanded an immediate response.

When he lifted her onto the side of the pool she knew he

was tempted. For a moment he moved between her thighs, took her breasts in his hands. Then, as she trembled at his touch, he took one swollen nipple into his mouth, tugging on it with his lips and tongue until she was throbbing all over.

Each nipple received the same treatment, and by the time he sprang out of the pool and drew her to her feet she could barely stand. Her legs were weak and her senses felt as if they were as taut as violin strings. Seeing him, aroused and magnificent, was no turn-off. Springing proudly from its nest of hair, his manhood was as powerful as he was.

'Come,' he said, taking her hand and starting towards the house, and when she stumbled he turned back and swung her into his arms. '*Pobrecita,*' he whispered, his lips finding the vulnerable curve of her nape. 'Am I going too fast for you? I want this to be as good for you as it is for me.'

Alejandro carried her into the house and up the stairs, apparently uncaring that neither of them was wearing any clothes. Abby, who had admired the soaring ceiling of the reception area earlier, barely noticed it now. The exquisite crystal chandelier, whose lamps had been muted since their arrival, shone down on a scene more unreal than any she had ever imagined. But Abby's eyes were focused on Alejandro, on the lean, aristocratic lines of his dark face as he mounted the stairs without effort, taking them to the upper floor.

His bedroom was just as opulent. A huge square bed occupied a central position, with several chairs grouped beneath the wide windows. There were shaded lamps and concealed lighting up near the moulded ceiling, but Alejandro turned off the switch as he came through the door. Now only two or three bulbs provided a subtle illumination, highlighting the satin coverlet, creating shadows in the corners of the room.

When he laid her down, the coverlet clung to her shoulders. 'I'm wet,' she protested, but Alejandro's response was merely to stretch his length beside her on the bed.

'I know,' he said, one hand playing sensuously across her stomach and sliding briefly down between her thighs. 'I can feel it here.'

'That—that wasn't what I meant,' she got out breathlessly, and he smiled.

'I know,' he said again. 'But our skin will dry soon enough. Between us we will generate enough heat to drain the pool, *no*?'

Abby quivered. 'Alejandro—'

'Relax,' he told her softly, bending to bestow a line of kisses that followed the passage of his hand. With the utmost patience, he eased her shaking legs apart and licked her with obvious enjoyment. 'You are as delicious as you look,' he added, sliding back to share his explorations with her, and she could taste the spicy heat of her arousal on his tongue.

Her head swam as he continued to kiss her, but he seemed determined to prolong her delight. Every inch of her flesh— her limbs, her shoulders, her breasts—all received his sensual ministrations, and Abby reached for him mindlessly, eager to end this torment that was both a pleasure and a pain.

But Alejandro was in no hurry, and it was only when she captured him between her palms and caressed his silky length that he moaned in protest. '*Es inútil, cara,*' he whispered achingly. 'It is no good. I must have you.' And, easing her legs wider, he moved between her thighs.

And then swore.

Softly, but distinctly. The word he used was unfamiliar to her, but Abby knew it wasn't good. '*Caray,*' he added, less violently. 'I have left my wallet by the pool.'

Abby blinked, confused. 'Your wallet?' she echoed. 'But surely you can trust your—'

'That is not what I mean,' he said thickly. 'I have no protection here.' He raked back his hair with a savage hand. '*Mierda*, I will have to go downstairs.'

'Oh, no, please…' Abby thought she wouldn't be able to bear it if he left her now. 'It's all right,' she told him frantically. 'I—I can handle it. Just—just don't leave me, please.'

Now, two years later, lying chilled and sleepless in her bed, Abby acknowledged for the first time that Alejandro hadn't been totally to blame for what had happened next. How had she blotted that out of her mind? Oh, he hadn't been completely honest with her about the fact that he was still married, however unstable that marriage had been, or made any attempt to see her again after she'd gone back to England. But he had believed she was more experienced than she was. He'd probably imagined that she was taking the Pill.

Whatever, her words had evidently reassured him, because he hadn't hesitated any longer. He'd entered her in one swift thrust that had had her catching her breath. He'd been so big, so thick, he'd filled her completely. She'd been halfway to an orgasm before he'd started to move.

She hadn't known that then, of course. Her previous encounter had given her no reason to believe that there was more to sex than the excitement Alejandro had engendered this far. Even the undeveloped sensations she'd had when he'd pulled back, before surging into her again, had had her arching towards him more in need than expectation. The feelings that had been building inside her were tantalising but, she'd believed, unreachable. The incredible truth of her own sexuality had yet to dawn on her.

That it had, in such a fantastic fashion, had been all due to Alejandro, she admitted painfully. She recalled him kissing her and caressing her as he drove them both to the very peak of sensual fulfilment. He'd been sweating, she remembered, his eyes dark and passionate, gleaming as he'd shared her breathless climb. She'd cried out as she'd reached her climax, only seconds before he'd collapsed, shuddering, in her arms. And feeling his hot seed spilling inside her had renewed the feeling, sending her shattering into a million shards of light…

She shuddered now, the memories suddenly too painful to rekindle. Had she really been that frantic, that naïve, that desperate? She'd been like moulding clay in his hands, only far more responsive to his touch.

She expelled a long breath. Of course, at the time, she'd been too dazed to realise what had happened. Too pathetically grateful to him for showing her how incredible sex could be.

But then, he had been a master at the art of seduction, and she'd been a willing novice, eager to learn.

He'd made love to her again before he'd carried her into his shower and allowed the cool water to cleanse their sweating bodies. Then he'd collected their clothes from beside the pool, helped her to dress, and taken her back to the Esquivals. She'd known she should have told him she was leaving the next afternoon, but it would have sounded like begging. How could she pretend that what had happened had been the same for him as it had been for her?

It hadn't been until a few weeks after she'd got back to London that she'd discovered she was pregnant. By that time Edward and Lauren had come back from their honeymoon, and it had been a simpler thing to ask her brother who Alejandro really was. When Edward had told her he was married she'd been devastated. And when, a couple of weeks later, she'd miscarried the baby, she'd told herself it was all for the best.

Only it hadn't been.

Rolling onto her stomach, Abby let the hot tears seep into her pillow. Tragically, while she was in the hospital, she'd contracted an infection, and after spending several days flat on her back recovering from a haemorrhage she'd been told that it was unlikely that she'd ever conceive again.

Ross knew, of course. She'd had to tell him when he'd asked her to marry him. She hadn't told him how it had happened, of course, and she hadn't known whether to be glad or sorry when he'd confessed that he had no desire to have children anyway. Somehow she'd always imagined that one day she would be a mother, even if she had to adopt a child to satisfy the maternal instincts inside her.

And that was why she was so protective of her brother, she thought. Despite the considerable distance between them, she still felt responsible for him. It was the main bone of contention between her and Ross—or it had been. Now she wondered if she had any future with anyone, when it seemed obvious that she hadn't got over Alejandro as she'd thought...

CHAPTER FOURTEEN

ABBY had her chance to talk to Edward alone the next morning.

For once her brother was eager to talk to her. She knew it was because she'd had dinner with Alejandro the night before and Edward was eager to hear the outcome. But it hurt her that he could be so transparent. Didn't he care about her feelings at all?

Abby had already decided she was going home that evening. She'd rung the airport before going down to breakfast and had been both disappointed and relieved when she'd found she'd have no trouble getting on the flight. She was relieved because she wouldn't have to worry about seeing Alejandro again, but she was disappointed because her visit had solved nothing. Quite the opposite, in fact.

She knew it was cowardly to run away, but she couldn't help it. She couldn't bear to face Alejandro again, knowing what she knew now. Running away seemed the only answer; the only way she could hope to retain any dignity at all.

She was sitting on the patio, rehearsing what she was going to say to the Esquivals, when she heard Edward's uneven step behind her. His crutches rang against the tiles, heralding his approach, but she refused to acknowledge that she'd heard him. She wasn't sure what she was going to say to him, and knowing she was leaving that evening meant she couldn't be as frank as she'd have liked.

'Hey, you!' Edward exclaimed as he lowered himself onto the cushioned recliner beside her. 'Didn't you hear me coming?'

'I heard you.' Abby shrugged. 'Where's Lauren?'

'Lauren?' Edward blinked. 'I don't know. I think she's taking a shower. Does it matter?'

'It might.'

Abby was cool, and Edward seemed to realise that all was not as it should be. 'What's the matter?' he asked. 'Why are you giving me that dirty look? Am I in the doghouse?'

Abby hesitated before replying. Then she said quietly, 'You tell me.' She paused, and then went on, 'In fact, you might start by being honest with me for a change.'

Edward snorted. 'I beg your pardon. When haven't I been honest with you? I don't know what you're talking about.'

'Don't you?'

She arched her brows and Edward eyes narrowed, his expression changing in a flash. 'Oh, I get it,' he exclaimed. 'This has something to do with last night, doesn't it? Come on. Spit it out. What lies has Varga been telling about me now?'

Abby stared at him, suddenly realising what he was trying to do. Maybe, thanks to Alejandro, she was beginning to see her brother in a different light. Whatever, she suddenly knew that he was trying to make her feel defensive. He was hoping she'd feel threatened and blurt out everything Alejandro had said.

'Why should you think Alejandro would tell me anything about you?' she asked innocently now. 'I thought all I was supposed to do was persuade him to leave Lauren alone?'

'Well, it was, of course.' Edward scowled. 'But I know Varga better than you do. It would be just like him to try and turn you against me.'

Abby considered her words before replying. 'I don't understand,' she said. 'What could Alejandro possibly say to achieve such a thing?'

Edward's face showed a trace of colour, and he moved his shoulders impatiently. 'I don't know,' he muttered sulkily. 'He—well—he could have made a crack about the fact that I'm always broke.'

Abby felt the first twinges of apprehension. 'You're always broke?' she echoed blankly. 'What are you saying? That

Lauren's father doesn't pay you a living wage? I don't believe it.'

'Why not?' Edward was defensive now. 'You don't know what these people are like, Abby. They want to know how you've spent every cent. God, I can't even play the odds without Luis breathing down my neck every minute I'm at the track!'

'You go to the track?' Abby's heart sank. She had hoped that moving to America would cure him of that obsession. 'You do mean the racetrack, don't you? Oh, Eddie, you promised me you wouldn't—'

'Oh, for God's sake, get off my back, why don't you?' Edward was bitter. 'Don't you think I get enough nagging from my wife? I have to have some bloody entertainment. Being the Esquivals' son-in-law isn't all fun, I can tell you that.'

Abby drew a careful breath. 'And—Alejandro knows about this? About your gambling, I mean?'

'I thought he might.' Edward tried to sound offhand. 'Like he knows everything else.' He waited a beat, and then he added grimly, 'These people all stick together, Abbs. I bet the thugs at the track are friends of his.'

'What thugs at the track?'

But Edward was suddenly hooking his crutches beneath his arms, getting ready to leave her. 'It doesn't matter,' he said shortly. 'It's not your concern.'

'Do you owe Alejandro money?' she asked, dreading his answer, her hand on his arm preventing him from getting up 'Is that what this is really all about?'

Edward swore then, surprising her with his vehemence. 'No,' he muttered angrily. 'What do you think I am? If I owed Varga money don't you think the Esquivals would have heard of it?'

'I don't know.' Despite her own dealings with Alejandro—or perhaps because of them—she didn't think he would betray a confidence. 'So why are you afraid of him?' she persisted. 'It's not because of Lauren. I know that.'

'How do you know?' Edward wasn't prepared to back down so easily. 'You know nothing about us. About the problems we have. Did you know, for instance, that Lauren's desperate to have a baby? These people put a lot of store in having children. We've been trying for two years and I haven't been able to come up with the goods yet.'

Abby gazed at him. She remembered what Lauren had said on her arrival. About the fact that things had been difficult for them in recent months. She thought she knew what she meant now. And Alejandro had nothing to do with it.

'Maybe that's why she spends so much time with Varga,' Edward continued aggressively, and Abby's hand fell from his arm as his words gathered strength. 'How do I know he's not trying to give her a baby? She spends enough time with him, goodness knows.'

'Don't be ridiculous!'

But Abby pressed a hand to her stomach as she chided him. She was feeling sick suddenly, and it wasn't easy to hide her feelings either. Alejandro had assured her that it wasn't true that he had no interest in the younger woman. But could she trust him when she couldn't even trust her own brother?

'Why is it ridiculous?' Edward demanded now, staring at her suspiciously. 'That joker hates me, doesn't he? My God, what did the bastard say? Here I was, thinking you'd be having a cosy session getting it together with lover boy, and all the time you were pulling yours truly apart.'

Abby cringed at his accusation. But she couldn't allow him to get away with it without making an attempt to stand up for herself. 'So that *was* what you wanted,' she said, unable to keep the distaste out of her voice. 'You really did expect me to go to bed with Alejandro. But not because you suspected he was involved with Lauren. How much do you owe him, Eddie? You might as well tell me. I'm going to find out anyway.'

'I've told you, I don't owe him a cent,' retorted her brother harshly. 'All right, I may have asked him for a loan. But he wouldn't do anything to help me.'

'And you thought if I—if we—' Abby couldn't finish the sentence. 'You thought he might loan me the money.' Her face mirrored her contempt and she found it hard to look at him. 'Don't you know a man like Alejandro doesn't have to pay for it? Besides, wasn't it you who told me he was married, just to stop me from having any ideas about him myself?'

'I thought I was doing you a favour.' Edward hunched his shoulders. 'Anyway, why bring that up now?'

'Because it's relevant,' said Abby coldly. 'You use people, Eddie. You didn't want me to get involved with Alejandro, so you told him some cock-and-bull story that I was engaged. That is true, isn't it?' She could tell from his face that it was. 'I've only just realised what Alejandro meant when he asked me about my engagement. You let him think I wasn't interested in him.'

'Well, you weren't.'

'How do you know that?' Abby felt cold inside now, cold and disillusioned. 'You didn't think about me at all, only what was best for you. What's the matter, Eddie? Were you afraid I'd be looking over your shoulder every time you strayed out of line?'

Edward grunted. 'It wasn't that simple. This was a new start for me. I didn't want—I didn't want—'

'Me screwing it up?' Abby felt hurt now, and angry. 'But now you need my help so you thought you'd take advantage of me again?'

'No—'

'Yes.' Abby couldn't bear to look at him. 'You disgust me, Eddie. You really do.' She hesitated, and then, deciding she had nothing to lose, she added painfully, 'I was pregnant when you told your pitiful little lies two years ago. When you decided to—mess up my life, I was expecting Alejandro's child!'

'*No!*'

The awed whisper came from somewhere behind them, and for an awful moment Abby thought Alejandro had come upon them, unobserved. But then the realisation that it had been a female voice brought her instantly to her feet.

'Lauren,' she said weakly, as the younger woman moved out of the shade of the awning. 'I—I didn't realise you were there.'

'Obviously not,' said Lauren evenly, but her eyes had turned to her husband in open enquiry.

'How long have you been there?' demanded Edward, struggling to his feet and casting a killing glance at his sister. 'I don't know what you think you've heard, but Abby was just letting off steam because she's got to go home.'

Lauren ignored him, her gaze returning to her sister-in-law now. 'You said you were expecting Alejandro's baby,' she prompted, causing Abby's heart to plummet. 'I did not know you knew my mother's cousin so well.'

'She didn't,' said Edward shortly, scowling at his sister. 'He must have—had sex with her the night of our wedding. That was all it was.'

Abby flinched at his callous dismissal of her relationship with Alejandro. Yet wasn't he right? Hadn't she been as easy as he accused her of being? She hadn't even had the sense to insist that Alejandro used protection. She'd been so frantic, so mindlessly eager, so afraid that he'd change his mind.

Lauren was waiting for her reply, and Abby took a steadying breath before saying flatly, 'It was a mistake.' It let her brother off the hook, but what the hell? She didn't want his broken relationship on her hands, too. 'It should never have happened. I lost the baby just a few weeks into term.'

Lauren pressed her hands to her mouth. 'Oh, Abby,' she said, her eyes filling with tears. 'I am so sorry. You must have been devastated.'

Abby couldn't let her think that. 'It wasn't so bad,' she lied. 'It would have been hard for me to bring a baby up on my own.'

'Of course.' Lauren nodded. 'Now I understand about your broken engagement. Edward told us what had happened, but didn't tell us why.'

'No.' Abby had to force herself not to look at her brother. She'd suspected what he'd done, but it wasn't the same as having it confirmed in this way. 'And now, if you'll excuse me, I'd like to go and pack. I'm leaving this afternoon. I have to get back to England, you see.'

'But what about Alejandro?' exclaimed Lauren, staring at Abby through lashes still wet with unshed tears. 'You must tell him what happened, Abigail. He deserves to know the truth—'

'No!'

'Dear God, no!'

Edward and Abby both spoke at once, and this time her brother had her full support. 'You must not mention a word of this to Varga,' he snarled. 'Are you out of your mind? He'd never forgive her for not telling him. Can't you see that?'

'I think you are afraid that he might blame you, Edward,' declared Lauren in her clear, slightly accusing, voice. 'I was coming to tell you, *cara*. They have found the men who trashed our apartment. Alejandro had his suspicions after learning that you owed money to some people at Hialeah Park, and with his help the police were able to arrest the guilty ones.'

CHAPTER FIFTEEN

ABBY took a taxi to her own tiny flat in Notting Hill when she got back to London. She argued with herself that it was early morning, that Ross wouldn't want to meet her and miss taking his first class of the day. But what she really meant was that she didn't want her fiancé turning up at the airport; didn't want to spend the best part of an hour making small talk on their journey into town.

In actual fact she'd been deliberately vague about her plans when she'd spoken to Ross before leaving Florida. She told herself it was because she hadn't decided what she was going to do yet, but that wasn't really true. She knew she was going to have to find a way to break her engagement. And that wasn't going to be easy when, as far as he was concerned, nothing had changed.

But things had changed for her. She'd changed, she acknowledged, after paying the driver and rummaging through her bag for her keys. It wasn't just the relief of knowing that Lauren knew about Edward's gambling, or that Alejandro had known what her brother was doing all along. It was the realisation that, long before Alejandro's behaviour had been justified, she'd realised that her feelings for him were not going to go away.

Which was stupid when it was obvious that he despised her. He thought the only reason she'd let him touch her was to save her brother's skin. And it was too late now to tell him that she hadn't been thinking about Edward when she'd kissed him—even if he wanted to hear it. Their whole relationship had been dogged with lies and half-truths, and although it wasn't all her fault he was never going to believe her now.

Endearingly, it had been Lauren who had begged her not to

eave without seeing him. Lauren who had so easily explained her own involvement with Alejandro when she'd admitted she was receiving treatment to help her conceive. Alejandro had been paying her medical bills. She was desperate for a baby, as Edward had said, and she hadn't wanted to tell her parents or worry her husband when she knew they were short of cash.

Of course her brother had maintained he'd known nothing about it. Whether he had nor not, Abby didn't know, but it was a relief to know that Lauren still loved him in spite of his faults. She was even going to ask her father to loan them the money to pay off Edward's debts. And, although Abby guessed her brother was going to have some difficult times ahead, perhaps that was the only way he was going to learn.

If only they could all have such a happy ending, she reflected ruefully, inserting her key in the lock and pushing open the door. Surprisingly, there was no pile of mail in the hallway, as she'd expected, and as she went into the living room she heard the radio playing in the kitchen annex next door.

She didn't have time to panic, however. She had barely registered that there was someone in the flat before Ross put his head round the door. 'Surprise, surprise,' he said, evidently expecting her to be delighted. 'I had a free first lesson, so old Banks said I could come in later on.'

Abby dropped her haversack onto the floor. She'd left her suitcase in the hall and she had the unpleasant feeling that she was a stranger in her own home. How had Ross got in? To her knowledge, he didn't have a key. All right, perhaps she should have given him one, but this had always been the place where she could escape from everyone. It had been her bolt-hole ever since the house she'd shared with Edward had had to be sold.

Ross had come fully into the room now, and was advancing on her with arms outstretched. 'Hey, what's wrong?' he asked, his brows drawing together. 'I thought you'd be pleased to see me. I've got a pot of coffee brewing, and there's toast and bacon under the grill.'

Abby could hardly hide her revulsion. She'd been offered

bacon and eggs on the plane and she hadn't been able to eat them then either. She felt sick, not just with the change in time zones, but with apprehension. She so much didn't want to face this confrontation now.

Ross's arms dropped when he saw her expression. 'Oh, hey!' he exclaimed. 'I've been thoughtless, haven't I? You're not feeling well. What was it? A rough trip? The gales across the Atlantic can be murder. I remember once, when I was coming back from New York, we had to have our seatbelts on the whole—'

Abby held up her hand to stop him. 'How did you get in, Ross?' she asked, cutting him off in full flow.

'How did I get in?' Ross blinked. 'With my key, of course.' He pulled a face. 'I didn't break in, if that's what you're thinking. After I'd spoken to your brother, I had the bright idea of staying the night here.'

'You've been here all night?' Abby was incredulous. 'And how did you have a key to this place? I've never given you one.'

'No, well, I guessed that was just an oversight, so I had one made weeks ago,' said Ross comfortably. 'Now, aren't you glad I did? It wouldn't have been much fun to come home to an empty flat.'

Abby thought it would have been heaven, but she couldn't say that, so she said faintly. 'You say you've spoken to Edward?'

'Last night,' agreed Ross calmly. 'I wanted to speak to you, of course, but he told me you'd already left for the airport. I did think about coming to meet you at Heathrow, but this seemed the better option. I know you don't much feel like talking when you've come off a long flight.'

Abby took a deep breath. 'You shouldn't have bothered,' she said, trying to hide her frustration. It wasn't his fault that she'd made such a mess of her life.

'Well, take off your jacket,' he said now, evidently deciding not to press his luck by being too affectionate. 'Like I say I've got some coffee in the kitchen. I'm sure you'd like a cup.

'Not right now,' said Abby, unbuttoning her jacket almost automatically. And then, remembering what she was doing, she added. 'As a matter of fact, it's probably just as well you're here. We have to talk.'

Ross looked doubtful. 'Oh, I don't think we have time to talk about your trip now,' he said, glancing at his wristwatch. By my reckoning we've just got time to have breakfast together and then I'll have to go. I know I told Banks I'd be late, but we don't want to offend him, do we? I mean, especially when he was so understanding about you taking time off—'

'Ross, please!' Abby wished he would just shut up and let her speak. Didn't he realise she was on edge? She had virtually accused him of trespassing, for God's sake. Yet he happily went on trampling over everything she said.

'I'll get the coffee—'

'No!'

'No?' He looked confused. And then he noticed she wasn't wearing her engagement ring. 'Oh, Abby,' he exclaimed, don't say you've lost your ring? That was a very expensive ring, you know. I expected you to be more careful—'

'I haven't lost it,' she cried, scrabbling in her bag and bringing out the offending item. She held it out to him. 'That's what I wanted to tell you. I'm sorry, Ross. I'd have liked to give you more warning, but—well, I think you should take this back.'

Ross made no attempt to take the ring. 'You're not serious,' he said disbelievingly. 'You're tired. You don't know what you're saying.'

'Oh, I do.' Abby had never been so sure of anything in her life. 'I've thought about it and thought about it, and my feelings aren't going to change. I wish I didn't have to say this, but I can't marry you, Ross. I'm sorry.'

Ross's face was tight. 'This is your brother's doing, isn't it?' he said angrily. 'I knew I shouldn't have let you go out here.'

'You couldn't have stopped me,' said Abby, disliking his

proprietorial attitude. 'I thought Edward was badly injured and I had to go and see for myself.'

'That he wasn't,' said Ross sarcastically. 'Apart from that emotional stress you made so much of. For Pete's sake, Abby, don't be such a fool! We've got so much going for us: similar backgrounds, similar interests, similar jobs.'

And how depressing that sounded suddenly. Maybe she was being foolish. Maybe she'd never find another man as patient as Ross. Or another man who'd want a woman who couldn't give him children, she reminded herself painfully. But that was her tragedy, not his.

Whatever happened, she didn't love Ross. She knew that now. She'd probably known it even before she'd got on the plane to Miami. That was why she'd felt so strange, seeing his ring on her finger. She'd never intended to let things go so far.

Nevertheless, seeing Alejandro again had altered everything. Until then she'd been able to fool herself into thinking that what she'd felt for him had died along with their child. Now she knew it wasn't true. She'd never stopped loving Alejandro. She had hated him sometimes, but her real feelings had never changed.

'I'm sorry,' she said again now, putting the diamond ring down on the coffee table that stood between them. 'I'd like to be able to blame Eddie, too, but it's not true, Ross. He had nothing to do with my decision. I thought I loved you, but I don't. I like you. I like you a lot. But that's not enough to base a marriage on.'

He looked mutinous, but she noticed that he bent and picked up the ring and slipped it into his trouser pocket before he spoke again. 'So what now?' he demanded. 'Are you going back to Florida? I suppose your brother has finally persuaded you to settle over there.'

As if!

'Of course I'm not going back to Florida,' Abby answered. Her lips twisted. She doubted if she'd ever go to Florida again. 'I'll be going back to work next week. I expect we'll see one another in the staffroom, as usual. I'm hoping we can still be friends.'

Ross's face brightened. 'You're coming back to school?' he exclaimed. 'Well—of course we can still be friends.'

'Good.'

Abby was relieved, but she had the feeling Ross hadn't given up hope of her changing her mind. He probably thought she was just testing the waters. Perhaps it would be best to look for another appointment after all.

After Ross had gone, Abby collected her suitcase from the hall and loaded the washer. Then, going into her bedroom, she quickly stripped the bed. It was childish, she knew, but she couldn't bear the thought that Ross had slept there. She needed to make a fresh start, and clean sheets and pillowcases were a beginning.

And during the days that followed she did try to pick up the pieces of her life. Going back to work helped, so long as she could avoid any *tête-à-têtes* with her ex-fiancé. The children she taught, the teachers she worked with, were all reassuringly familiar, and she was soon caught up in the day-to-day activities of the school.

Only in her quieter moments, and when she got to bed at night, did she succumb to her emotions. She found herself remembering how she'd felt when she'd been pregnant with Alejandro's child. Not unnaturally, now she found herself wishing she could have had the baby. At least she would have had some part of him to love.

As she'd suspected, Ross had apparently decided that all she needed was a breathing space. When she encountered him in the staffroom he insisted on behaving as if it was only a matter of time before she took back his ring. She didn't know what he'd told his colleagues. She'd made it perfectly clear to her friends that the engagement was over. But Ross's skin was thicker, and he couldn't seem to accept that she wasn't going to change her mind again.

Perhaps that was her fault, too, she reflected, when she left work late one afternoon at the end of April to find Ross waiting at the gates. He'd known she'd stayed back that day to meet the parents of one of her students. And, although it was only a short walk from the school to her flat, he'd evidently decided to wait and give her a lift.

It was a pleasant afternoon. The almond blossom was out on the trees and Abby had been looking forward to the walk through the park that adjoined her square. Besides, she had no intention of giving Ross false hope by accepting his invitation. It had been thoughtful of him to wait, but he had to realise he was wasting his time.

'Everything okay?' he asked as she came through the gate, almost as if his waiting for her was still the usual thing. 'Who was it you had to see?'

'It was Shelly Lawson's parents,' said Abby, wishing she could just walk past him. 'What are you doing here, Ross? Did you have a meeting, too?'

'As if you didn't know,' he said, indicating his car parked on the street. 'Come on. I'll buy you a cup of coffee and a Danish. You look as though you could do with a break.'

Abby expelled a sigh. 'Ross—'

'Look, I know what you're going to say. I'd got no right to assume that you'd be glad to see me. But, hell, Abby, how long is this going to go on? It's already been five weeks!'

Abby shook her head. 'Go home, Ross. That's where I'm going. I'll see you tomorrow—'

'No, you won't.' To her astonishment, Ross grabbed her arm and prevented her from moving away. 'Like I say, I've been patient, but you've got to stop all this nonsense. I'm not going to be turned away like an unwanted toy.'

Abby stared at him incredulously. 'Ross, what do you think you're doing? Let go of my arm. You're hurting me.'

'Well, that's par for the course,' he said angrily. 'When you hurt people you have to expect to be hurt in return. You've made a fool of me, Abby, and I'm not going to stand for it. You're coming home with me and we're going to sort this out.'

Abby gasped. 'No.'

'Yes.' Ross started propelling her across the pavement. 'It's not as if there's anyone else. You ought to be grateful to me for taking pity on you. Everyone knows what a sad life you've led since Edward moved to the States and married that Spik!'

Abby's jaw dropped in horror at his words, but before she could respond a long shadow fell across the path. As Ross had been wrestling her towards his car another vehicle had cruised to a halt behind it. A tall, dark-clad individual had thrust open the door and uncoiled his long length from behind the wheel.

'Is something wrong, Abigail?'

The dark, disturbing tones were unmistakable. Managing to wrench her arm free of Ross's grasp, she turned and saw the Cuban standing negligently beside his car. His elegant suit and the shadow of stubble on his jawline were in stark contrast to Ross's sports coat and bearded countenance. Yet, despite the hollows beneath his eyes, Alejandro had never looked better or more familiar.

'Who the hell is this?' demanded Ross, unwilling to lose the initiative, and Alejandro inclined his head towards the other man.

'I am the cousin of the—er—Spik who married Abigail's brother,' he replied, and Abby's heart sank at the knowledge that he had heard Ross's coarse indictment. 'And you must be—'

'Abby's fiancé,' Ross put in aggressively, the colour in his cheeks the only indication he felt any shame.

'Her ex-fiancé,' she corrected him tersely. Then, managing to recover her composure, she turned to Alejandro, 'I must apologise for Ross's rudeness. He's not usually so crass. I'm afraid he's had a trying day.'

Alejandro's eyes were disturbingly intent as they appraised her. 'And you, *cara*,' he said softly. 'Have you had a trying day, too?'

'A long one,' she said. Then, nervously, 'What are you doing here, Alejandro? Did Eddie ask you to come and see me?' She paled a little at this thought. 'Nothing's wrong, is there?'

'With your brother, no,' Alejandro assured her smoothly. 'He is able to walk again and he is hoping to return to work in a few weeks.' He glanced thoughtfully at Ross before adding, 'I went to your flat, but it was unoccupied. Your neighbour directed me here.'

'You went to her flat?' echoed Ross, his face darkening ominously. 'I don't know who you are, friend, but you've got no right to turn up uninvited at Abby's door.'

'First, I am no friend of yours,' said Alejandro, his mouth twisting distastefully. 'And, as Ms Leighton was trying to get away from you when I arrived, perhaps you are no friend of hers either. In any event, if I understand her correctly, you are no longer her fiancé. I suggest you do as she says and go home.'

Ross snorted, stiffening his spine and squaring up to the other man. 'And if I don't?' he said challengingly, evidently spoiling for a fight. 'What are you going to do about it?'

Abby stifled a groan. 'Please, Ross,' she said desperately. 'Do as he says. I'll—I'll speak to you tomorrow. Alejandro's an old friend. I'll be perfectly all right with him.'

Ross's brows drew together. 'How old a friend?' he asked suspiciously. 'How long have you known him? Why haven't I heard about him before? Did you meet him when you went to Edward's wedding? Is that what he means when he says he's related to Edward's wife?'

Abby sighed. 'Well—yes. If you must know.' She cast a glance towards Alejandro, hoping he wasn't listening to this. She lowered her voice. 'Ross, please, this is not your business.' She took a breath. 'Just go home.'

But Ross seemed indifferent to her pleading. 'How well do you know him?' he demanded. 'Am I allowed to ask that?'

'I think you have asked enough,' broke in Alejandro, and Abby knew he'd been listening all along. 'How well Abigail and I know one another is our business. As she says, it is no concern of yours.'

'It is if you know the bastard who got her pregnant and abandoned her,' retorted Ross outrageously, his words chilling

Abby to the bone. 'I guess you didn't know about that,' he added, as Alejandro rocked back on his heels as if someone had struck him. 'Yeah, Abby thinks people here don't know what happened, but she's wrong. She'd just come back from her brother's wedding, and you don't spend over a week in the gynaecological ward of the hospital without people talking. I guess she lost the kid, but I'm not supposed to know. All she told me was that she couldn't have children, and that suited me. I get enough of them at school every day. I never wanted any of my own.'

CHAPTER SIXTEEN

ABBY didn't wait to hear any more. She wanted to die, she thought sickly. She could think of nothing she wanted more than for the earth to open up and swallow her. She didn't want to live. She'd didn't want to see the shock and horror on Alejandro's face. Nor did she want to have to defend herself to him. He hadn't known, he wasn't meant to know, and that was how she'd wanted it to stay.

Turning on her heel, she almost ran across the road, uncaring of the traffic, which fortunately was light. She could hear Ross calling her name, but she didn't answer. Right now she couldn't bear to look at him. How could she have ever contemplated spending her life with him?

She reached the park unharmed and set off swiftly along the path. She expected one or both of them would follow her, but if she could get into her flat she needn't open the door to anyone. All right, Ross had a key, but there were bolts at the top and bottom of the door. Surely one of them would respect her privacy. What had happened was her loss, no one else's.

As for Alejandro, she couldn't imagine what he must be thinking. He would probably consider the fact that she had been expecting his child without telling him a betrayal of the highest order. Yes, he'd been married, but Edward's story now was that he and his wife had been virtually separated. Would she have told him in those circumstances if she hadn't lost the child?

The answer was probably no, she conceded. After all, as far as she'd been concerned Alejandro hadn't wanted to see her again. They had had a one-night-stand, the kind of thing she would never have dreamed she was capable of. And, because of that, she'd spent the last two years trying to come to terms with it.

She'd thought she'd succeeded. She'd really thought that her relationship with Ross was all she wanted out of life. Or perhaps all that she deserved, she concluded sadly. She'd thought she was depriving him of the chance to become a father, before realizing it suited him far better than her.

But what had he hoped to gain, blurting it out like that? Did he suspect Alejandro was the man involved? And was it true that everyone at the school knew she'd had a miscarriage? My God, had Ross discussed her with the other teachers? Had they all speculated about who might be to blame?

Abby was feeling more and more desperate. It was a nightmare, she thought. How could she ever face her colleagues again? And Alejandro... Well, she couldn't even bear to think about how Alejandro might be feeling. Was he angry? Did he hate her? Or was he just full of contempt for the way she'd behaved?

To her surprise—and to her relief—she reached her flat without incident. There was no sign of Ross's car in the square; no sleek black Mercedes like the one Alejandro had apparently hired. Perhaps they'd both decided she wasn't worth bothering about, she thought painfully. It wouldn't be the first time she'd been on her own.

She was making herself a cup of tea with shaking hands when she heard a key rattling in the lock. But she'd bolted the door behind her, and now she was glad she had.

'Abby!' shouted Ross, evidently putting his mouth close to the letterbox. 'Open the door, Abby. I want you to see what that bastard has done to me.'

Abby groaned. What now? she wondered wearily. Didn't Ross realise he'd said enough? Besides, as far as Alejandro resorting to physical violence was concerned, she didn't believe it. He was far too laid-back to get into a fight over a woman he hardly knew.

'Go away, Ross,' she called, going out into the hall so he

could hear her. 'I don't want to speak to you now. In fact, I don't know if I'll ever want to speak to you again.'

'Oh, come on, Abby.' Ross was harsh. 'We both know you need me. Just because Varga's given me a black eye doesn't mean he's going to be hanging about.'

Abby's fingers trembled as she tore back the bolts and wrenched open the door. But when Ross would have stepped inside, she blocked him, her eyes turning incredulously to his face.

He was right. He did have the makings of a black eye. The skin around his eye looked puffed and sore, his eyelid swelling ominously over the pupil.

Her lips parted. 'Alejandro did this?' she breathed incredulously, and Ross took a belligerent stance.

'You needn't look so pleased about it,' he snapped. 'Now, are you going to let me in? I think you owe me an explanation. Who is this man Varga, for God's sake? Don't tell me he was the father of your child?'

Abby's mouth closed. 'I'm not going to tell you anything, Ross,' she said quietly. 'And as far as owing you an explanation is concerned, you can't be serious. You shamed me. You embarrassed me and humiliated me. And don't pretend you were doing it for my own good. I've never felt so awful in my life.'

Ross's jaw jutted. 'Well, you had to know sooner or later. People aren't fools, Abby. Women particularly gossip about stuff like that. I mean, they know something happened to prevent you from having children. What other explanation could there be?'

Abby stiffened. 'How do they know I can't have children?' she demanded.

Ross sighed. 'Well—I may have said something,' he muttered unwillingly, and Abby sagged against the door.

Then, straightening, she said, 'I meant what I said before. Go away, Ross. Go away, and don't ever come near me again.'

She slammed the door then, leaning back against it as hot tears flooded her eyes. My God, and she'd thought she could trust him. He was just like Edward. He said whatever was necessary to get his own way.

She had papers to mark, but she dumped them all on the table in the living room, too distressed to attempt any kind of work. Instead, she rescued her tea and curled up on the couch, trying not to think about the future. Her whole world seemed to be tumbling about her and she didn't know what she was going to do.

She supposed she ought to feel something about Alejandro's treatment of her ex-fiancé. Some gratitude, perhaps, that he had felt compelled to act in her defence. But she couldn't help wondering if he hadn't acted as he had because he'd been so furious about what Ross had told him. Alejandro was a proud man, and he probably thought she'd made him look like a fool.

Whatever, she thought wearily, there was nothing she could do about it now. The only thing she could hope for was that rumours didn't start flying about the school. If anyone had seen the fracas—and there had still been students about, she remembered—it would soon reach the ears of the head teacher.

She must have been sitting there for over an hour when someone knocked at her door. Ross, she thought tiredly. When was he going to realise their relationship was over? But then she remembered she hadn't bolted the door again after he'd left earlier. Surely if it had been Ross he'd have used his key first and argued later.

Getting to her feet, she went to the hall door and called, 'Who is it?' It was almost dark, the bright day giving way to an overcast sky. She seldom opened the door at this time of the evening without identifying her caller. It wasn't wise to take any chances, however unlikely danger might be.

'Abigail?'

Alejandro's voice was low and unmistakably weary. As soon as she heard it she knew she'd been half hoping that he might come. But why? she asked herself. Whatever had brought him to London, Ross's words had destroyed any empathy between them. And besides, after the way he'd behaved on his boat, she was foolish if she thought he was here because of her.

But she couldn't ignore him. Not when he had taken the trouble to come to the flat. So, abandoning any hope of disguising the tears she'd shed earlier, she rubbed brisk hands over her cheeks and opened the door.

She didn't know what she'd anticipated. Maybe some evidence of the fight he'd had with Ross. Perhaps she'd half expected him to be sporting a black eye, too. But apart from his drawn expression, which had not been there earlier, he looked much the same as he'd looked before.

Alejandro had been propped against the wall beside the door, but now he straightened. 'Do you want me to come in?' he asked, and she realised he wasn't angry with her.

'I—of course,' she said, stepping back so that he could move past her. She closed the door and followed him into the living room. 'So—this is a surprise.'

Alejandro turned in the middle of the living room floor, his size immediately dwarfing the apartment. 'But not a pleasant one,' he said, and she knew he'd noticed her swollen eyes. 'Is Kenyon here? I would like to apologise to him.'

Abby gasped. She couldn't help it. 'No, Ross isn't here,' she said, her heart sinking at the realisation that she'd been completely wrong about his visit. She swallowed. 'What made you think he was?'

'I saw him come here,' said Alejandro simply, his dark eyes shadowed. 'I waited for him to come out again, but his car is still downstairs.'

'His car is still downstairs?' Abby blinked. 'I didn't know that.' She licked her lips. 'He left here over an hour ago. Perhaps the car wouldn't start. That happens sometimes.'

'Ah.' Alejandro sounded thoughtful, but she could tell from his expression he wasn't convinced. 'Or perhaps he thought I would not come here if I thought he was still with you,' he remarked consideringly. 'Your fiancé is a determined man, *cara*. He does not give up.'

'He's not my fiancé,' insisted Abby tersely. But she suspected that was exactly what Ross might have done. He would never expect Alejandro might feel the need to apologise to him. Nevertheless, leaving his car outside was such a childish thing to do.

Alejandro shrugged, his shoulders moving freely beneath the fine wool of his jacket, and Abby couldn't help remembering that evening on his yacht. When he'd held her in his arms. When he'd danced with her and pretended he was going to seduce her. She wished he had. But, like Ross with his car, he'd only been playing a game.

'He's not here,' she repeated, when it seemed obvious something more was expected of her. She hesitated. 'I'm sorry if what he said upset you. You weren't ever supposed to find out.' She wrapped her arms about her midriff, unknowingly protective. 'I know I should have told you when it happened, but—well, I thought you were a happily married man.'

'And this would be because Edward told you?' suggested Alejandro harshly, his expression hardening as he spoke of her brother's involvement in the affair. He swore softly. 'I hope you know now that he was lying to you, Abigail. As he lied to me when I told him I wanted to see you again.'

Abby looked dazed. 'You wanted to see me again?'

'What else?' But Alejandro did not sound as if the knowledge pleased him. 'And I am not talking about today, this week, this month, even this year. *Por l'amor de Dios*, Abigail, I would have come to you after our first meeting. Edward knew that. I told him. I said I wanted to see you again, and he—' His lips twisted. 'He laughed in my face.'

Abby stared at him. 'He laughed?' She couldn't believe it.

'As good as,' said Alejandro dismissively. 'He told me you would not want to see me again. That you already had a fiancé. That you were planning to get married. That you would not welcome me turning up to complicate your life.'

Abby was aghast. 'I didn't know you wanted to see me again,' she got out at last, unable to cope with the implications of Edward's treachery right now. 'Besides, you were married,' she said again. She hesitated a moment, and then added, 'Eddie didn't lie about that.'

'What is that expression? He was economical with the truth.' Alejandro made an impatient gesture. 'I gather he did not tell you that I had already filed for divorce? Maria and I— that was my wife's name—we had separated some weeks before your brother's wedding. Lauren and her parents knew this. I find it hard to believe that Edward did not know this, too.'

'Perhaps he did.' Abby put an unsteady hand to her head. 'I had no idea that he had even spoken to you. When I asked him about you, all he said was that you already had a wife.'

Alejandro swore. 'I believe you,' he said harshly, and Abby noticed how pale he'd suddenly become. 'So—when I was imagining that your behaviour had been unforgivable, you were obviously thinking the same of me?'

'Something like that,' murmured Abby, hardly able to take it all in. Then, noticing that he was swaying on his feet, she indicated the sofa behind him. 'Won't you sit down?'

'*Gracias.*' Alejandro needed no second bidding. With a gesture of apology he sank down onto the sofa and expelled a long sigh. 'Forgive me,' he said. 'It was a long flight and I am tired. I fear the consequences of not sleeping for more than twenty-four hours are catching up with me.'

Abby glanced towards the kitchen. 'Are you thirsty?' she asked anxiously. 'Can I get you something to drink?'

'Sitting down will do it,' Alejandro assured her, loosening the buttons of his jacket. He looked up at her with a brave attempt at a smile. '*Sí*, I am feeling much better already.'

Abby doubted he was. Now that he was below her eye level she could see the shadows of weariness in his face. Dear God, what had Edward said? she wondered. How had he dismissed her behaviour at the wedding? Had Alejandro really thought that she had just been playing a game?

'Are you not going to join me?' he asked now, shifting along so that she could sit beside him. But Abby didn't trust herself to be so near to him when her emotions were in such a chaotic state. Despite what he'd implied, she wasn't sure what he expected of her now.

Instead, she perched on the arm of the chair opposite as she tried to make sense of all he'd said. It seemed apparent that he had come all this way just to see her, but was it to clear the air between them or because he wanted something more?

Before she could say anything, however, Alejandro spoke again. 'I do not blame you for being wary of me,' he observed bitterly. 'What did you think I was doing two years ago, I wonder? You must have believed I had only been amusing myself at your expense. Did you think I seduced you for fun? That I took you to my father's house and made love to you to satisfy some perverted need to prove I could?' His expression mirrored his disgust. 'It was not like that, Abigail. I am not like that, whatever you may have heard.'

'I know that now,' she murmured helplessly. 'And Ross is the first man I have been engaged to. There was no one else.'

'*Cristo!*' Alejandro swore violently. 'No wonder you hated me, *cara*.' His lips twisted. 'Perhaps you hate me still.'

'No.' Abby pushed herself up from the chair, unable to sit still under the accusation burning in his eyes. 'And I don't think you really believe that.'

He arched his dark brows. 'Why not?'

'Well…' Abby struggled to find the right words. 'That night on the yacht—'

'Ah, *sí*.' Alejandro's eyes darkened. 'Let us talk about that night on the yacht. Let us get all the—what do you call it?— the baggage out of the way first. Then we can talk about what is really important, hmm?'

Abby swallowed. 'If you like.' She glanced towards the kitchen once more. 'But, if you don't mind, I think I will make another pot of tea. I—I—' *Need it!* 'I'm thirsty.'

'*Bien.*'

He rose to his feet then, and she was taken aback to find him towering over her again. 'No—I mean, you can stay here,' she said hurriedly. 'Rest. Relax. I won't be long.'

'Do not ask me to wait here like a spurned lover,' he exclaimed huskily. 'Let me come with you. I promise I will not get in the way.'

Abby quivered. His entreating words stirred every nerve in her body, and it was all she could do not to ask him to explain himself there and then. But she had to keep her head, she reminded herself. Just because Alejandro was here that did not mean all her troubles were over.

He was waiting for her answer, and with a little shrug she said, 'Well, all right. But, I warn you, it's nothing like the kitchens you're used to.'

'Do you think I care?' His voice was suddenly thick with emotion, and he put out his hand to tuck a strand of her hair behind her ear. Then he trailed his fingers across her cheek with evident concern. 'You are not going to cry again, are you? I know that man—Ross—must have hurt you, but in his defence I have to say I think he does care about you very much.'

Abby found it difficult to speak, but, steeling herself against the tears that were still pressing, she said, 'I hurt him, too. He's not a bad person. He just—well, I'd rather not talk about it right now.'

'I understand.'

But Alejandro's mouth had tightened a little and his hand dropped to his side. Abby told herself she was glad. She couldn't bear for there to be any more mistakes. And if he had come to England to see her, what had taken him so long?

He stood at the entrance to the tiny kitchen as she plugged in the kettle and prepared a tray. At his nod she added an extra cup, and then waited nervously for the kettle to boil.

'You have lived here long?' he asked politely after a moment, and she explained that she had moved here when Edward went to live in the United States. She didn't add that it had always been her bolthole when the world had seemed an unfriendly place—like when she'd come back from Edward's wedding, for example—or that she would never be able to stand in her kitchen again without seeing him propped against the counter as he was now.

'And Ross?' he probed. 'Did he live here, too?'

'No!' Abby was very definite about that. 'Ross has his own place. A house not far from here.'

Alejandro absorbed this, the lines at either side of his mouth deepening as he continued, 'And do you still care about him? Despite the fact that you are no longer together—?'

'We're no longer together because I don't love Ross,' said Abby tensely, glad that the kettle boiled at that moment, giving her something to do to avoid his eyes. She hesitated. 'Do you—do you take sugar in your tea?'

'I will take it however you want to give it to me,' replied Alejandro roughly. Then, as if he couldn't stand to wait any longer, he said, 'You do know why I was so—so angry that night. The night on the yacht,' he elaborated shortly. 'I really thought you were only there because Edward had asked you to intercede on his behalf.'

Abby's hand shook a little as she placed the teapot on the tray. 'That was why I accepted your invitation,' she admitted unsteadily. 'But then, you know that. That was why you decided to—to teach me a lesson.'

Alejandro uttered an exclamation. 'Is that what you think?'

'I don't blame you,' said Abby hurriedly. 'Until then I'd only had a suspicion that Eddie wasn't telling me the truth. But I got it out of him later. Too late, sadly, to tell you.'

Alejandro's brows drew together. 'But you left the next day,' he exclaimed in protest. 'I had a business meeting in Tallahassee that I couldn't avoid, and by the time I got back you had gone. Your brother took great pleasure in telling me that, whatever I had told you, he didn't need me any more. Luis—proud fool that he is—had agreed to cover your brother's debts. For Lauren's sake, you understand? She still loves him—and the child which is even now growing inside her.'

Abby caught her breath. 'Lauren's pregnant?'

'With God and the IVF clinic's help,' agreed Alejandro drily. 'She is so happy that I do not think my friend could

have forbidden her anything. Including his help for that un-
grateful son-in-law of his.'

Abby trembled. 'I'm so happy for her,' she said. 'For them
both.' She paused. 'When did they find out?'

Alejandro shrugged. 'Lauren had suspected for some time,
I think, but she wanted to wait until she was sure before breaking the news to her husband and her parents.'

'I see.'

'In any case, that is not why I came,' he said shortly. Then,
moving forward, 'I will take the tray.'

'No.' Abby put herself between him and the counter. 'I can
manage. Please. Just go and sit down.'

'And if I do not?' His eyes were on her deliberately averted
face. *'Cara.'* His voice deepened. 'This is not going to work.
How long do you think you can keep me at arm's length? I
came to see you. Only you. To see if there was any chance
that you might give me another chance.'

'Another chance?' The tray forgotten, Abby turned to him.
She shook her head. 'But why did you wait so long?'

Alejandro shook his head. 'Why do you think?'

Abby blinked. 'Edward?' Though she couldn't see how her
brother could have had anything to do with it.

'Of course Edward,' said Alejandro heavily. 'You have to
know that I assumed you were still engaged to this man Ross.
Por Dios, you were wearing his ring. I had no doubt this time
that he did exist.'

Abby stared at him. 'So how did you—?'

'Find out your engagement was ended?' he finished harshly.
His lips twisted. 'For reasons best known to himself, but I
suspect because Lauren asked him to, Edward admitted that
you had broken up with your boyfriend. But that was not until
yesterday, you understand? Until then I believed what you had
told me. *En realidad*, I thought you probably hated me.'

'I never hated you,' she said huskily. 'Oh, Alejandro, I don't
know what to say.'

'Me, either,' he said, straightening and running the knuckles of one hand down her flushed cheek. 'Can you ever forgive me?'

'Forgive you?'

'For not being there when you needed me,' he said, and she expelled a sigh.

'But you didn't know.'

'And you think that is a good enough excuse? You do not think I should have tried to see you again?'

'In the circumstances, probably not,' she conceded tremulously. 'You have to remember, I had just learned that you were married.'

'*Dios!*' Alejandro's eyes were dark with emotion. 'Such a tangled web!'

'And mostly of Eddie's making,' said Abby unhappily. 'He was so desperate to make it on his own. Since our parents died I've been more like a mother than a sister to him, and he resents it.'

'You know him too well, *cara*,' said Alejandro softly. 'You know his faults and his weaknesses whereas I do not. And because of that I assumed you were just like him. When you returned to Florida, all I could think about was finding some way of hurting you as you had hurt me.' He groaned. 'What a stupid, arrogant fool I was.'

'Alejandro—'

'No, listen to me, *cara*. You have to know how it was.' He blew out a breath. 'You see, this was not the first time your brother had found himself in financial difficulties since he came to the States. A year ago—the details are not important now—I agreed to help him, mainly because Lauren asked me to. But on this occasion—' He made a negative gesture. 'I refused.'

Abby turned horrified eyes towards him. 'Did he return the money?'

Alejandro sighed. 'That is not important, as I have said.'

'But did he?'

Alejandro hesitated. 'Some,' he admitted at last. 'The

money was not an issue, *cara*. Edward needed to realise he was living beyond his means.'

Abby shivered. 'You knew about those men at the track, didn't you? The ones who broke into their apartment?'

'When you told me what had happened, I suspected,' he agreed. 'And your arrival had been so convenient.'

'I thought Eddie had been badly hurt,' protested Abby weakly. 'I had no idea—'

'No.' Alejandro had moved a little nearer as she was speaking, and now his fingers linked caressingly around her wrist. 'You were worried about him. I know that now. At a guess, I'd say he let you think he was badly injured because he knew how you would feel. If I did not know for a fact that the other driver had been drinking, I would have to wonder if Edward had not caused the accident himself.'

Abby looked down at his fingers, brown against her paler flesh. 'If only I had told you about the baby,' she said huskily, unable to think of anything else when he was touching her. Besides he deserved to hear the story from her lips, not the garbled version Ross had vented on him. 'I wanted to tell you, but—well, you know what I thought. And then, when I miscarried—' She broke off, her voice wobbling revealingly. 'It was as if it was never meant to be.'

'And I knew nothing about it,' said Alejandro grimly. 'Edward should have told me.'

'He didn't know.' Abby was glad she could tell him that, at least. 'No one knew. That is, I thought they didn't. If what Ross said is true, I've been fooling myself for almost two years.'

'But you told him?' Alejandro ventured, his breath warm against her temple.

Abby shook her head. 'Not about you, no.' She paused. 'Just that I couldn't have children. I had no idea he suspected the truth.'

'*Sí.*' Alejandro said the word heavily. 'I knew you were upset when you ran away.' He waited a beat and then went on, 'But I should not have taken my frustration out on him. He was the catalyst, but not the offender. That was my role.'

'No!' Abby lifted her head to stare up at him with tear-washed green eyes. 'It wasn't your fault. It wasn't anybody's fault. Not even Edward's. If I'd been honest with him perhaps he'd have been honest with you. Who knows?'

'You are a very forgiving woman,' said Alejandro, gazing down at her. He lifted his hands to rub them almost possessively up and down her arms. 'Do I dare to hope that you might forgive me also?'

'There's nothing to forgive.' Abby was intensely conscious that there were only inches between them now, and her heart was beating faster every minute. 'Besides,' she added softly, 'Now that you know the truth, you must also realise that there is no future for us.'

'*Que?*' His reaction was violent. His hands gripped her upper arms with unwarranted strength and there was no mistaking the angry confusion in his eyes. 'What do you mean?' he demanded, practically shaking her in his desire to make her see sense. 'I thought— Surely I cannot have been wrong all along? I thought you cared for me—at least half as much as I care for you.'

'I do—'

'Then—'

'Wait.' Abby's lungs felt as if they were labouring. 'Alejandro, my feelings are not the most important thing here.'

'No?' He looked both puzzled and frustrated now. 'You cannot doubt that I care about you. I love you, Abigail. I have loved you ever since that morning you scrambled out of the Esquivals' swimming pool at my feet.'

Abby closed her eyes against his dark enchantment. It would be so easy to give in, so easy to delude herself that love would be enough. It wasn't. He had proved that by waiting over an hour before coming to see her tonight. He had been stunned by Ross's revelations. He had needed time to come to terms with what the other man had said.

'You forget,' she said with difficulty, 'I can't have another baby. I love you, but I know you want children of your own. For heaven's sake, you're your father's eldest son. When Ross told you—what he told you—you were shattered. I was there, Alejandro. I saw it in your face.'

'What did you see?' Alejandro wouldn't let her go when she tried to pull away from him. 'Did you see distress? Disappointment? Or did you see my pain at your devastation? Can you honestly say what you saw in my eyes?'

Abby was uncertain. 'You can't deny you took a long time to come to the flat.'

'You think it did not hurt me, too?' he demanded. 'You think I can hear that the woman I love has lost my child without feeling totally devastated myself? *Cara*, I needed time to come to terms with it. I admit it. But not because I had any doubts about how I felt.'

Abby shook her head. 'I don't know if I can believe you.'

'Why not?' He gathered her into his arms, pressing his forehead to hers. '*Por Dios*, Abigail, I cannot live without you now. You are my life, my future. You are all I care about. What use would there be for me to marry another woman when the only woman I want has admitted she loves me?'

Some time later, Abby stirred in the rather cramped surroundings of her bed to find Alejandro sound asleep beside her. He had been exhausted, she thought, stretching out a hand to push a lock of silky dark hair back from his temple. But not too exhausted to show her that he meant what he said. He loved her. The unbelievable was true. He loved her. And he didn't care that she was unable to give him another child. They could adopt, he'd told her gently, when she'd persisted in labouring the point. If that was what she wanted. For himself, she would be his wife. She was all he needed.

'What are you thinking?'

Unbeknownst to her, Alejandro's eyes had opened and now he was watching her with a sleepy amorous gaze. She was immediately conscious of the fact that the sheet had fallen away to reveal the rounded swell of her breasts, but although she blushed a little she didn't attempt to hide herself.

'I was thinking how much I love you,' she told him honestly. 'And I was also thinking that this bed isn't really big enough for you.'

'This bed is perfect,' Alejandro contradicted her softly, rolling nearer to bury his face between her warm breasts. 'I hope you are not suggesting that I should return to my hotel? Apart from anything else, it is—' he screwed up his eyes to look at the clock on her bedside table '—two o'clock in the morning. And I am so comfortable here.'

Abby's lips tilted. 'You don't really think I want you to go, do you?' she asked, as he lifted his head to nuzzle the curve of her neck. She wound her arms about his neck. 'I'm just finding it very hard to believe, that's all.'

'Believe it,' he told her fiercely. 'We are going to spend every night together from now on.' He grimaced. 'Whatever your brother has to say about it.'

Abby pulled a rueful face. 'I think he'll be surprised.'

'I do, too, though not perhaps as surprised as you, *cara*. He knew it was in his best interests to be honest with me. Perhaps he has realised that I can be of more use to him as a brother-in-law than an enemy.'

'Oh, Alejandro!'

'"Oh, Alejandro,"' he teased her, mimicking her outrage. Then his lips found hers with sudden ardour, his leg straddling her thigh so that she was left in no doubt as to his arousal. *'Te amo, querida,'* he murmured, whispering to her in his own language. 'Do you know how much I love you? How much I need you? You are my soul. The very meaning of my existence.'

His tongue slipped between her teeth then, finding the vulnerable contours of her mouth with hungry passion. One hand slid into her hair, the other cupping her bottom, holding her close against him.

'Tell me,' he said, his voice thick with emotion. 'Tell me you love me also. Then perhaps I will let you get some sleep.'

EPILOGUE

ABBY and Lauren were cooling off in the spa bath when Alejandro arrived home.

'Your husband is early,' observed Abby's sister-in-law uneasily, hearing the car, and Abby didn't correct her. But the truth was Alejandro was usually home early. He'd told her he resented every minute he spent away from her.

'I hope I am not interrupting anything,' he remarked a few minutes later, strolling out onto the deck that was steaming after the recent rainstorm. He had shed his tie, but he was still dressed in the suit he'd worn to his office. Although Abby was sure he must feel the heat, he looked as cool and dangerously attractive as ever.

He smiled at his cousin, but it was Abby who held his attention. Circling the tub, he bent and bestowed a lingering kiss on her mouth. Lauren shifted a little awkwardly, but Alejandro had no inhibitions. *'Hola, cara,'* he said, one hand straying sensuously across his wife's bare shoulder. 'Do you mind if I join you?'

Abby, who was used to her husband's outrageous behaviour, hid a smile, but Lauren had been born of more modest genes. 'I must be going,' she said hastily, reaching for the towel she had placed strategically beside her. She gave Alejandro a nervous look. 'Katie will have woken from her nap by now, and you know she doesn't like it if I'm not there to give her her juice.'

Abby reserved judgement. Catriona—Katie—was Edward and Lauren's small daughter. At eighteen months old, she was as pretty and feminine as her mother. Unfortunately, she was also spoiled, by both her parents and her grandparents, and she was becoming quite a tyrant.

'*Oh, por favor!*' Alejandro pretended to be devastated. 'Do not let me drive you away, *pequeña*.' He glanced down at his wife as he spoke, however, and she saw the wicked humour glinting in his eyes. 'Surely there is room in the tub for three?'

Lauren's lips tightened, and for a moment she looked disagreeably like her mother. 'I am sorry,' she said stiffly, clearly waiting for him to leave so that she could get out and wrap herself in the enveloping folds of the towel. 'I am sure you and your wife would prefer to be alone.'

Alejandro would have continued to tease her, but a look from his wife deterred him. 'You may be right,' he murmured, brushing his lips across Abby's head before heading for the sliding doors. 'If you will excuse me, I will go and get changed.'

However, as he entered the building another sound invaded the heat-laden air. A baby's cry, swiftly hushed, had him casting a wry backward glance at his wife.

'No,' he said imploringly, but Abby was already getting to her feet, climbing out of the pool, wrapping a towel about her nakedness with an innocent disregard for Lauren's feelings.

'Yes,' she said, catching up with her husband in a few barefoot strides. 'It is his teatime.' She had fastened the towel sarong-wise under her arms, and now she caught Alejandro's arm in a possessive grasp. 'It serves you right,' she added in an undertone, pressing against him. 'You were teasing Lauren mercilessly. You know how she feels about bathing in the nude.'

'She did not have to worry,' Alejandro assured her drily as they entered the spacious living room. 'She should know by now that I am not interested in looking at her naked body. I merely thought it would have been fun for us all to enjoy the tub together.'

'No, you didn't,' Abby contradicted him, but then he turned the tables on her by loosening the towel and gathering her into his arms.

'Tell me you are not going to spend the next hour feeding

our son,' he demanded pleadingly, burying his face in the damp hollow of her neck. 'I want you all to myself.'

'Hardly an hour,' murmured Abby, a catch in her voice. 'Darling, I'm going to lose the towel completely if you don't let me go.'

'I do not want to let you go,' he informed her thickly. '*Ah cara, quiero hacerte el amor!*'

'And I want to make love with you, too,' responded Abby, who had learned quite a bit of Spanish in the past couple of years. 'But Antonio is hungry and my breasts are aching.'

Alejandro closed his eyes. 'Lucky Antonio,' he muttered, and then, opening them again, he helped her adjust the towel once more. 'I hope he realises what I am sacrificing for his sake.'

Abby dimpled. 'I am sure he does,' she murmured. Then, more soberly, 'And we are so lucky to have him.'

'Hmm.' Alejandro pulled a wry face. 'I know. Although I sometimes think that if you had not been so sure you would not conceive again we might have taken more care than we did. I never intended us to have a baby just eighteen months after we were married.'

Abby smiled. 'But you're glad we have him, aren't you?'

'Our son?' Alejandro cupped her face between his hands. '*Querida*, you have no idea how proud I felt when you told me you were carrying our child. And watching him grow inside you…' He pressed a kiss to the corner of her mouth. 'That was—indescribable.'

The baby's cry could be heard again, and although the nursemaid was doing her best Abby knew that he would not settle until she had fed him.

'I won't be long,' she promised, escaping from her husband's arms with real regret. 'And afterwards—'

'Afterwards I will make up for lost time,' Alejandro assured her huskily. He stepped nearer. 'I suckled at your breasts long before he did,' he added, his hands straying irresistibly to the fullness outlined beneath the towelling. Then, restraining himself, 'Now I will see our cousin off the premises before she dies of embarrassment.'

Abby's laugh was soft and intimate. 'Don't be long,' she said. 'Oh, and by the way, she told me that Edward has finally finished paying off his debts. Whatever you say about Luis, he is not as soft as he appears. I think he and Edward are going to be good for one another.'

'Let us hope so.' Alejandro cupped her cheek. 'But I have to tell you, right now it does not interest me greatly.' Antonio's cry was becoming a little more urgent and he scowled. 'I have other matters to contend with,' he observed, glancing into the hall, where the stairs rose to the upper floor. 'Go and feed our son, *cara*. He sounds almost as impatient as I am.'

Abby started towards the door, but his voice caused her to glance round once more. 'I love you,' he said simply, and Abby's heart turned over.

'I love you, too,' she whispered. '*Te quiero, Alejandro. Tu eres mi vida.* You are my life.'

Modern Romance™
...seduction and
passion guaranteed

Tender Romance™
...love affairs that
last a lifetime

Medical Romance™
...medical drama
on the pulse

Historical Romance™
...rich, vivid and
passionate

Sensual Romance™
...sassy, sexy and
seductive

Blaze Romance™
...the temperature's
rising

27 new titles every month.

Live the emotion

2 FREE
books and a surprise gift!

We would like to take this opportunity to thank you for reading this Mills & Boon® book by offering you the chance to take TWO more specially selected titles from the Modern Romance™ series absolutely FREE! We're also making this offer to introduce you to the benefits of the Reader Service™—

- ★ FREE home delivery
- ★ FREE gifts and competitions
- ★ FREE monthly Newsletter
- ★ Exclusive Reader Service discount
- ★ Books available before they're in the shops

Accepting these FREE books and gift places you under no obligation to buy, you may cancel at any time, even after receiving your free shipment. Simply complete your details below and return the entire page to the address below. *You don't even need a stamp!*

YES! Please send me 2 free Modern Romance books and a surprise gift. I understand that unless you hear from me, I will receive 4 superb new titles every month for just £2.60 each, postage and packing free. I am under no obligation to purchase any books and may cancel my subscription at any time. The free books and gift will be mine to keep in any case.

P3ZEA

Ms/Mrs/Miss/Mr ....Initials....................................
BLOCK CAPITALS PLEASE

Surname ....

Address ....

....

....Postcode...............................

Send this whole page to:
UK: FREEPOST CN81, Croydon, CR9 3WZ
EIRE: PO Box 4546, Kilcock, County Kildare (stamp required)